LORD OF
THE DESERT

NINA BRUHNS

MILLS &
BOON

All the characters in this book have no existence outside the imagination of
the author, and have no relation whatsoever to anyone bearing the same name
or names. They are not even distantly inspired by any individual known or
unknown to the author, and all the incidents are pure invention.

First published in Great Britain 2011
Harlequin Mills & Boon Limited,
Eton House, 18-24 Paradise Road, Richmond, Surrey TW9 1SR

© Nina Bruhns 2010

ISBN: 978 0 263 88001 4

89-0311

Harlequin Mills & Boon policy is to use papers that are natural, renewable
and recyclable products and made from wood grown in sustainable forests.
The logging and manufacturing processes conform to the legal environmental
regulation

Printed an
by Litogra

Nina Bruhns credits her gypsy great-grandfather for her great love of adventure. She has lived and traveled all over the world, including a six-year stint in Sweden. She has two graduate degrees in archeology (with a speciality in Egyptology) and has been on scientific expeditions from California to Spain to Egypt and the Sudan. She speaks four languages and writes a mean hieroglyphics!

But Nina's first love has always been writing. For her, writing for Nocturne™ is the ultimate adventure! Her many experiences give her stories a colourful dimension and allow her to create settings and characters that are out of the ordinary. She has garnered numerous awards for her novels, including the prestigious National Readers Choice Award, three Daphne du Maurier Awards of Excellence for Overall Best Mystery-Suspense of the year, five Dorothy Parker Awards, and two RITA® nominations, among many others.

A native of Canada, Nina grew up in California and currently resides in Charleston, South Carolina.

She loves to hear from readers and can be reached at PO Box 2216, Summerville, SC 29484-2216, or by e-mail via her website at http://www.NinaBruhns.com.

This book is offered in fond memory of
Bengt Birkstam
a man of honor, wisdom and humor.
anhh d̲t r n

Chapter 1

I have seen him in his every outline,
Avoiding his pain, with no turmoil in him.
—Recited by the priestess at the Opening
of the Mouth and Eyes Ceremony

Present day
The Nubian Desert, Upper Egypt

The first time she saw him, he took her breath away.

Gillian Haliday would never forget that fateful moment as long as she lived. And that, it seemed, could be for a very, very long time....

* * *

Dawar, Gillian's mount for the day, pawed the hot Egyptian sand and pranced restlessly as she tethered him in the stingy shade of a date palm. It was noon and her sisters had just bounced up in the Land Rover to share lunch and a much-needed break from a long morning's work.

"What is it, boy?" she murmured, stroking Dawar's silky muzzle to soothe him. He was probably just as thirsty and tired as she was. Signaling to her assistant, Mehmet, to take over the horse's care, she headed for the ruins of an ancient temple of Sekhmet, where her sisters were spreading the picnic rug.

But something…she wasn't sure what… brought her to a halt. The fine hairs on the back of her neck prickled.

Raising a hand to shield her eyes from the glare of the blazing sun, she squinted and turned in a full circle to look around.

To the east in the distance shimmered the graceful, muddy curve of the Nile River, banked by a narrow parallel band of lush green fields. The vivid green ended abruptly in the harsh browns and blacks of the West Bank landscape.

The rough dirt track that served the few intrepid farmers, thieves and archaeologists who ventured to this side of the river cut its shallow twin ruts, hugging the edge of the fields like a child terrified to stray too far from its mother's hand. From the track, the land began a gradual upward slope for about three-quarters of a mile, where it was blocked to the west by the rugged, towering sandstone cliffs of the *gebel*. It was there, hidden deep in the forbidding shadows of the cliffs, that the realm of the dead, the famous tombs of the ancients, could be found, and just below, the scattered vestiges of their holy temples.

The *gebel* marked the western border of the Nile Valley, the distinct limits of civilization—ancient and modern—and the universally recognized line beyond which anyone who valued their life dared not venture.

"Hey!" Gillian's sister Gemma called out to her. "You snakebit or what? Get over here and help."

Gillian tried to shake off the weird feeling still coursing through her body like a hum of electricity. "Be right there!" she called back cheerfully. All morning she'd looked forward to sharing a meal with her sisters. It happened all too rarely these days.

But the creepy feeling wouldn't leave her alone. It was like she was being watched….

Following where the feeling led, her gaze was drawn upward. All the way up to the crest of the *gebel* above.

She gasped, not believing what she saw.

A huge black stallion stood very still at the apex of the vertical cliffs, his elegant ears pricked in her direction. Backlit against the bright yellow orb of the sun, the stunning Arabian's coat gleamed like black obsidian, hauntingly silhouetted, every muscle in his body rippling with power.

Not what she had expected. Her breath tried to ease out. But then caught again, arrested by the sheer strength of his presence. He was magnificent!

Impossible that the stallion could be wild. Not in this region, not for centuries. And yet, he appeared to be just that. Feral. Untamed. *Au savage.* She could tell with a single glance, this beast had never felt the bit between his teeth.

It might have been the blistering noonday heat, or perhaps her exhaustion after the grueling hours of the morning's trek, but it seemed to Gillian that the creature was actually staring at her. Deliberately watching her.

Her heartbeat jumped. And despite the hundred-degree temperature, a shiver tingled over her arms.

Suddenly, he reared, shaking his splendid head, his thick mane and long tail flying as his forelegs pumped the heat-shimmering air. *Good lord.* There was no doubt whatsoever that this was a stallion. The sight of him, wild, rampant and unfettered, sent heat blazing through her cheeks.

"My God," she murmured, then spun to wave at her sister. "Look! Do you see that?" She pointed up at the cliff.

Gemma paused in her unpacking of the luncheon sandwiches from a cooler strapped to the tailgate of the Land Rover. "See what?"

"There! Up on the *gebel.*"

They both glanced upward. But the only thing now at the top of the rocky cliff was the blazing sun above it.

The stallion was gone.

Gillian frowned. "But—he was just there!"

"Who was just where?" their other sister, Josslyn, asked, emerging from the temple ruin and striding up to the Land Rover. She removed her cloth hat and whacked it against her thigh, raising a cloud of dust. Joss was the oldest sister, an archaeologist.

"There was a wild horse up on the *gebel*," Gillian told her excitedly. "An intact stallion," she added, ignoring the lingering remnants of her blush.

Joss clucked her tongue as she took a bottle of water from Gemma. "No wild horses in this part of Egypt, jelly bean."

"Oh, but you should have seen him! He was amazing."

"It must have gotten loose from one of the nomad encampments upriver," Gemma said logically, and handed Gillian an icy bottle of water, too. All three sisters poured a few drops of water onto the ground. "I'm sure its owners will be by soon, looking for it."

Gillian shook her head. "Trust me, that stallion has no owner."

Both of the other women glanced at her, brows hiked.

"Well, then," Joss said, leaning in with hushed drama in her voice, her eyes twinkling, "you must have seen al Fahl."

Gillian blinked, then grinned. "Al Fahl? You mean the shape-shifter from the crazy story villagers tell their kids to scare them into behaving?"

"You know very well the native legends aren't crazy," Gemma scolded mildly. "Many of them have a basis in—"

"Fact." Joss mimicked the word, rolling her eyes. "More like a load of bull."

This was an old argument. Gemma was a cultural anthropologist, a specialist in traditional Nubian stories and lore. But for scientist Josslyn, only hard, quantifiable facts could convince her of anything. Thank goodness Gillian was a historian, and usually able to avoid being dragged into their spirited anthropological debates.

"Al Fahl." She pursed her lips, vaguely recalling this particular legend. "The ghost stallion."

"An evil shape-shifter," Gemma elaborated,

"who gallops from village to village stealing away young women—"

"*Virgins*," Joss corrected acidly.

"—*and* men, to become human servants—"

"*Sex* slaves," Joss sang.

"—*servants* to the powerful demigod Seth-Aziz—"

"In his underground palace," Joss completed, snorting as they settled onto the rug they'd laid in a sliver of shade next to the crumbling temple wall. "Yeah, right."

"Seth-Aziz…" Gillian pondered, her gaze landing on a weathered depiction of the lion-headed goddess Sekhmet, known for her taste for human blood. "Isn't he supposed to be some kind of vampire?"

"Oh, my God. Not you, too," Joss moaned. "There's no such thing as a freaking vampire!"

"How can you be sure?" Gemma insisted. "Every single known culture on earth has had a vampire myth. That's quite a statistical anomaly if they don't actually exist," she argued, playing to the one thing that would shut Joss up.

Gillian dropped her jaw as the three of them

spread the picnic on the rug. "*Every* known culture?"

Gemma wagged her finger at Joss. "Explain *that,* smarty pants."

Joss chuckled, taking a sip of water. "Uh. Hello? How about the boundless capacity of mankind to invent lame stories to explain every little bump in the night?"

Gemma let out a huff of outrage. "Says *you,* who routinely invents lame explanations for why people threw out piles of broken junk five thousand years ago. Like that's any mystery. It's *broken!*"

Rather than be offended, Joss just laughed. She'd heard it a hundred times before. "Whatever. Besides, what would Gillian's wild horse be doing working for a vampire, anyway?"

"Not a horse. A man who turns into a horse. A shape-shifter."

"Stallion," Gillian corrected, glancing up at the cliff top. "A magnificent wild stallion who lures unwitting virgins with his untamed beauty."

"And his magnificent untamed coc—"

"Josslyn Haliday!" Gillian and Gemma erupted in unison, scandalized. Okay, not really. More like greatly amused. No doubt Joss was right about his lure.

"Still…" Joss tossed them each a wrapped pita sandwich. "Better watch out, jelly bean. If it is an intact stallion you saw up there, wild or not, he's probably after your little mare."

Gillian unwrapped her sandwich and grinned. "In that case he'll be sorely disappointed. I'm riding Dawar today. A gelding."

Gemma winked, playfully bumping shoulders with her. "Better be careful anyway, baby sister. Al Fahl might just be after *you!*"

Joss snickered. "Then he'll be *really* disappointed."

Gillian let out a mock gasp, giving her sister a teasing poke in the arm. "Don't worry, I'll just send him *your* way."

They stuck out their tongues, making faces at each other as their laugher echoed off the *gebel,* the hot desert air ringing with their merriment.

God, how she loved being with her sisters again!

They had been apart far too long. With

Gemma's new teaching position at Duke University in the States, Joss's work for the Royal Ontario Museum in Toronto, and Gillian's own doctoral studies in Oxford, England, it seemed the only time the three of them ever saw each other was when they were all in Egypt at the same time doing research.

Egypt. The country where they'd grown up, traveling with their Egyptologist father who had determinedly excavated tomb after tomb as he'd pursued his dark demons after their mother's death two decades ago, not far from here. Their father had returned obsessively to this remote place on the West Bank, a bit north of the first Nile cataract, season after season, year after year. Eventually he had abandoned their South Side Chicago home for the country he'd loved, until he, too, had deliberately walked into the endless sands to die, and be forever close to the woman he'd loved too much to ever get past her loss.

Gillian would never forgive him for that. For giving up. For leaving his three daughters alone in the world. For taking the easy way out. Life was a gift. It shouldn't be squandered.

She sighed and rested her back against the sandstone blocks of the temple wall, eating her pita and letting her gaze meander over her happily chatting sisters and the stark, rugged desert landscape that surrounded them. People often asked how they could bear to come back to the unforgiving country that had robbed them of both parents. Not to mention that this place was rife with terrorism and unpredictable political unrest. But the answer was simple.

All three sisters loved Egypt with a passion that flowed in their blood like the waters of the Nile. Despite the glaring cultural differences, despite the very real dangers and despite the heartaches it reminded them of, more than anywhere else in the world, Egypt was their home.

"Hello? Earth to Gillian."

Her sisters were looking at her, smiling with indulgence. How long had they been calling her? She shook off her melancholy and smiled back. "Sorry. Must have dozed off." She did have a habit of drifting off into the twilight zone, sometimes for hours at a time. That's what came of a childhood without TV, or even electricity for the most part. Usually it was a happy occupation. Fantasies could be very entertaining….

"Dreaming about your handsome stallion?" Josslyn teased. "Too bad he's a mythical beast and not a real man."

"*Tcha.* Like I have time for real men." Gillian polished off her last gulp of water and climbed to her feet. Not that she wouldn't enjoy male company once in a while. But lately her studies had taken up every waking minute. "Enough of this lollygagging. Got work to do."

"But you look exhausted," Gemma said, putting a hand on her arm. "Come back to the villa with me and take a nap. You can hunt for your stupid old grave later, when it's not so blasted hot."

"No can do," she said, giving her sister a quick peck on the cheek. "I'm too close. Today's the day, I can feel it in my bones."

Gillian had come to Upper Egypt for a very specific reason. She'd been hired by a good friend of one of her Oxford tutors, a British viscount, Lord George Kilpatrick, to lay to rest a disturbing ancestral skeleton. In 1885, the heir to the family title had died somewhere between here and the second cataract, the same year the famous General Gordon had perished. Lieutenant Rhys Kilpatrick had been a member of the Nineteenth Hussars, the relief force that arrived in Khartoum two days too late to save the day, resulting in Gordon's ignoble demise at the hands of al Mahdi. Afterward, a rumor had reached England that the lieutenant had become enmeshed in some bizarre Egyptian cult sometime before that, had in fact deserted his column and joined the enemy, and had not been killed heroically at the Battle of Abou Klea at all, as reported in official military accounts.

Gillian's task was to find Lieutenant Kilpatrick's grave marker or other solid evidence and, once and for all, quell the malicious whispers that had persisted longer than a century.

"Really, sweetie, you do look all in," Gemma persisted stubbornly. "If the grave is there today, it will certainly still be there tomorrow."

Gillian grabbed a fresh bottle of water from the cooler. "Oh, it's there, all right. I've recognized some of the unexcavated tombs Father sketched in his notebook. And he mentions this very temple." She gestured to the ruins behind them.

"Egypt is littered with unexcavated tombs and crumbling temples," Joss reminded her. "And Father was notorious for muddling locations because he didn't always keep his notes up-to-date."

"Besides," Gemma said, "I don't see how that fuzzy reference to a mysterious Kilpatrick inscription in Father's diary even refers to your lieutenant's grave. He was supposed to have died in the Sudan, two hundred miles south of here!"

"Which is why no one's ever found it," Gillian said, undaunted. She gave them a cheerful wave and went off to fetch Dawar and Mehmet.

Mehmet, her guide-slash-assistant, was a skinny kid of indeterminate preadolescent years with a winning grin and extremely light fingers. Handily, he seemed to know every soul both honest and shady living in the Nile Valley, from Luxor to the Sudan. And probably beyond. Gillian figured if she ended up having to sneak over the border into forbidden territory to complete her job, the kid would be invaluable.

"*Y'alla*, Mehmet," she called, rousting him from where he sat on his haunches under the sheltering ledge of a large boulder. "Let's go."

He didn't budge.

Puzzled, she looked over at him. And saw he was staring up at the *gebel*, a strange expression on his face.

Ah.

"You saw him, too?" Thank goodness, she hadn't been hallucinating after all. She smiled. "Don't even think about it, kid. That stallion's not for you. He'd have you for breakfast."

Without moving his eyes, Mehmet slowly shook his head. "*La'*. No, miss. This one, he is for you."

"Me?" Her brows flickered, torn between a frown and laughter. "I don't think so."

Mehmet's soulful brown eyes finally met hers. There wasn't a speck of his usual adolescent mischief or humor in them. "It is al Fahl," he said.

The frown finally won out. The boy had the street smarts of a grown man and spoke English almost flawlessly, so she had to remind herself he was a simple villager, uneducated beyond the fourth grade at the most, his head filled with primitive local superstitions. That was why Gemma came here to do her anthropological research. The whole area was rife with the stuff. Ghost stallions, shape-shifters and vampires, oh, my.

Mehmet reached for the amulet he always wore on a leather thong around his neck. A wedjat, or Eye of Horus. Except it was the right eye instead of the usual left-facing one. She'd always attributed that oddity to the fact that he hailed from Qurna, a village on the West Bank, usually associated with the land of the dead. The right eye was the one that Set-Sutekh, god of the hot winds, chaos and darkness—and the West Bank—had torn in jealous hatred from his brother Horus-Ra. The left eye—some sort of cult symbol, she thought.

"Mehmet, surely you don't believe in such things," she said, careful not to sound disrespectful, just in case. "Al Fahl isn't real."

For a split second, his gaze held an emotion that might have been pity as he looked at her. Then it vanished just as quickly. His eyes cleared and he bounced up, his usual energetic self.

"This is Egypt, miss," he said with a grin, in his distinctive clipped and rolled accent. "Very mysterious. Who can say what is real and what is mirage?"

Chapter 2

I enter to see him.
—Opening of the Mouth Ceremony

Lord Rhys Kilpatrick slipped quietly through the stately silver portal to the luxurious temple within Khepesh Palace and made his way through the hushed darkness toward the inner sanctum, the holy of holies where the Opening of the Mouth and Eyes ceremony was taking place.

He was late.

"Oh, Seth-Aziz, hear us!" a trio of dulcet

female voices chanted. Their sweet tones echoed softly off the gleaming silver pillars and walls of the inner sanctum.

Damn. The ritual was almost over. Seth's inner mummy case had already been raised to stand upright before the priestess Nephtys. The precious metal and lapis lazuli adorning the elaborately carved obsidian sarcophagus from which it had been lifted winked and shone from the light of a hundred fragrant altar candles, reflecting the glittering starlight of ten thousand diamonds that radiated down from the midnight-blue curved ceiling overhead. The ritual never ceased to impress him, nor did the splendid setting. Whatever else, Seth-Aziz had exquisite taste. His five-thousand-year-old tomb—now expanded into the sumptuous underground palace called Khepesh where they all lived—was amazing in every aspect.

"Your purification is the purification of the great god Set-Sutekh," the priestess Nephtys murmured, swinging a censer, walking around the mummy case four times, smudging it with smoking ambergris and myrrh.

Luckily, Rhys's attendance was not critical.

Or even needed, really. The monthly ceremony to awaken the demigod from his full-moon slumber depended only upon the priestess and her two *shemat*s, or acolytes. Nephtys was the one who possessed the power to raise the dead, not Rhys.

"May the god open the mouth and eyes of his loyal follower, Seth-Aziz, so he may walk and speak with his body before the great nine gods in the magnificent Palace of Khepesh, and drink the blood of his humble servants," they chanted.

Nevertheless, Rhys made it a habit to be there when Seth awoke each month upon the second setting of the sun after the full moon, on the chance his services were required. One never knew what his friend would be in need of upon awakening. A special food. A particular book. A beautiful woman. A willing sacrifice for his bloodlust…which thankfully happened but once a year anymore.

Rhys halted a respectful distance from the altar that overflowed with lotus flowers surrounding a goblet of wine. Nephtys sent him a smile, then held up a snakelike implement topped by a ram's head, and with the tip touched first the mouth, then the eyes of Seth's man-shaped coffin.

"I have opened your mouth and your eyes with this blade of iron that came from Set-Sutekh, with which the mouths and eyes of all the demigods are made to taste and see. May your *ka* arise, my brother, and reawaken to life!"

The priestess and her *shemat*s leaned in, raising their arms in supplication. This was Rhys's favorite part. The real magic.

From beneath the lid of the mummy case a misty shape began to materialize, taking on form and solidity as it stepped free of the trappings of death. The shape slowly resolved into a tall, handsome, black-haired man, regal of bearing and stern of aspect. Rhys's lord and master, and best friend for the past hundred and twenty-five years.

The vampire demigod, the High Priest Seth-Aziz, come back to life.

Or at least his *ka*. In Egypt, a man had three souls, the *ka,* the *ba* and the *akh,* each with a different function. Few believed the whole of the man-god's being still lived, but rather that it was only his solid soul, his *ka* body double, that was called back from the land of the dead to feed upon the blood of the living. Seth-Aziz was like no other who dwelled in Khepesh. Just two of his kind remained in the whole of Egypt. The last of a dying breed…

It was all a mystery to Rhys, but the spell had worked every month now for nearly five thousand years. Nevertheless, all in attendance let out a sigh of relief mingled with awe when Seth's eyes fluttered open and focused softly on the priestess.

"Sister," Seth greeted her, his voice strong and sure. "Ever the loveliest of sights to chase off dreams of the underworld."

Nephtys leaned forward and gave Seth an affectionate kiss on his smooth, perfect cheek. "Dreams or nightmares, *hadu?*"

The Guardian of Darkness shrugged non-committally. "It is what it is." He turned to Rhys, stepping forward to put his hand on his shoulder, his flesh now as firm as Rhys's own. "And my loyal Englishman, here to welcome me back as always."

"I am your humble servant, my lord."

Seth chuckled. "You are neither servant nor particularly humble, Lord Kilpatrick, yet it pleases me to hear you say so." He returned Nephtys's kiss on the cheek, then turned to usher Rhys away between the rows of silver, papyrus-shaped pillars. "How are things up in the mortal world, my friend? Anything urgent to deal with?"

Rhys bowed his head in parting to Nephtys and winked at the two pretty *shemat*s, then matched his stride to Seth's, heading out through the courtyards of the temple compound and into the grand hall beyond the temple portal.

"Things are quiet, but simmering," he reported.

"So you think the war with Haru-Re is heating up again," Seth observed with neither excitement nor anger.

"Yes. I suppose we're overdue," Rhys said philosophically. "Ray likes to rattle his chains every century or two."

The animosity between Seth-Aziz and his perpetual enemy, Haru-Re—or Ray, as he liked to call himself these days in what he thought was a clever pun—had been going strong for five millennia, an extension of the original war for supremacy between their leaders, the powerful rival gods Set-Sutehk and Re-Horakhti, begun at the dawn of Egyptian civilization. After the fall of the ancient gods, their immortal followers—or *shemsu netru* as they were called—remained on earth, still locked in the ebb and flow of battle. Although *immortal* was a bit of a misnomer. Under certain circumstances it was possible for even a demigod to succumb to death permanently. In fact, through battle and magic, and the one secret, fatal weakness of vampires, nearly all the demigods who had once flourished had been destroyed. And as the leaders had died, so had their *shemsu*. Today, only two cults, or *per netjer* as they preferred to be called, still remained—those led by Seth and Haru-Re.

"There is a rumor Ray may be lurking somewhere nearby," Rhys said. "Shahin's spies are due back tonight with a report."

Sheikh Shahin Aswadi was captain of Seth's cadre of guards, and a good friend to both Rhys and Seth.

Seth's face went stony. "Have him shore up our defenses. Nephtys must be protected at all costs."

Originally one of Haru-Re's captive slaves, a princess from a far northern island, Nephtys had been rescued from the enemy and adopted by Seth's father in the days when they were still young and mortal. From her lowly beginnings, she had risen to become a powerful priestess. Today she was the only one alive with the knowledge to transform mortal to immortal.

Haru-Re was obsessively determined to get her back.

"We must prepare ourselves for the battle. And increase our number," Seth ordered as the two of them strode into the Great Council Chamber.

Rhys reluctantly agreed. It was a well-traveled, if dangerous, road. After the untimely death of Haru-Re's priestess, he now had no means of converting either *shemsu* or the menial his own human servants called *shabti,* and had taken to stealing Seth's. Thank goodness the enemy had not yet resorted to capturing the shape-shifters of Khepesh. But it was a concern, making it necessary for them to step up recruitment of initiates.

If it were up to Rhys, there would be no *shabti* at all in Khepesh. They were the unlucky ones, robbed of all mind and will. It was a cruel and unnecessary fate to impose on anyone. But unlike Rhys, not every mortal wished to serve the Lord of the Night Sky, nor willingly paid the price of immortality....

"Our number may be increasing sooner than you think," Rhys said, reminded of the situation that was currently causing him worry. "A mortal is getting dangerously close to discovering the eastern portal of Khepesh, in your old tomb."

Seth halted in front of the enormous ebony council table, now empty. "Just what we need. Who is this mortal? Grave robber or archaeologist?"

"Neither. I am told it is an historian seeking to document a more recent grave."

"A grave? Whose?"

"My own."

Seth's brows shot up. *"Yours?* By Osiris's member, why would they be looking for that?"

Rhys sighed. He'd been fearing this very thing since he'd made his original fateful decision in 1885. "Apparently, the Kilpatrick family wishes to put an end to certain persistent rumors regarding my desertion from the British army."

Seth's lip curled. "Your unsavory past catches up with you at last, my friend. Well, then. This meddlesome mortal must disappear, mustn't he? Who is this man destined to be my newest initiate?"

"He," Rhys answered with a calculating smile, "is no man. It is a woman."

What Mehmet said was true, Gillian thought, taking a last lingering glance up at the *gebel* where they were headed. The whole country was a cipher, impossible to puzzle out. *One of its many charms,* she silently ventured as she gathered her pack together.

Mehmet whistled loudly as he hurried to fetch Dawar, and by the time she'd swung into the saddle, his own small donkey had trotted up and he'd mounted, ready to lead on.

It was the hottest part of the day, so they took

it slow and easy on their climb back to the foot of the towering ochre-and-beige-striped formations of the *gebel*. The old expression, "Only mad dogs and Englishmen go out in the noonday sun," had originated in places like this, and for good reason. The sun and heat could literally kill anyone who didn't take ample precautions. Unfortunately, all three sisters' university schedules precluded doing research anytime other than summer break. Normally, Gillian would have heeded Gemma's advice to wait until the relative cool of late afternoon to continue her search. But today she was too anxious, certain that the Kilpatrick inscription her father had mentioned in his survey notebook was close by. Very close by.

Excitement bubbled within her at the prospect of finding it and completing her mission with a good result for her client. Historians didn't have a lot of exciting job options. Teaching was about it. Which was fine. She loved history, and that was part and parcel of the profession. But success here could lead to other fascinating historical detective work during future summer holidays.

"Miss," Mehmet called over his shoulder as he pulled his donkey to a stop. The donkey didn't have a name. Mehmet claimed it would be silly. "You didn't name your car, did you?" he'd cheerfully argued. Actually, she had; but she'd prudently decided not to get into that debate. "While we rested," he continued, "I saw a shadow in the rock face. There." He pointed up. "I think it's an opening."

Gillian had learned on the first day working with Mehmet always to trust his instincts. She suspected he often knew much more than he let on, and was in his own way leading her to a tomb, ruin or other site he thought she might find interesting, without prompting sticky questions he'd rather not answer about the origins of that information. Egypt's most lucrative export had always been illegally obtained antiquities. Tomb robbing was a mainstay for many West Bank locals. The whole subject could bring Josslyn to a frothing frenzy of outrage over the loss of valuable archaeological data due to thieves' complete disregard for anything other than saleable goods. Mehmet was undoubtedly connected in a big way to the trade. But unlike her sister, Gillian believed in quietly educating those involved. Hiring them for jobs such as this was a strategy far more likely to succeed in the long run than yelling at them or calling the corrupt antiquities cops, who would slap one hand while taking *bakshish* from the other.

"An opening? In the rock?" she asked. "You think it's a tomb?"

"Maybe yes," he said, nodding as he glanced back at the *gebel,* avoiding her eyes.

She cocked her head. "Then let's check it out."

"Yes. Good." He looked almost nervous as he spurred his donkey forward up the increasing slope.

She wondered why. Maybe this was a rival village's territory and he was worried about repercussions. Usually such animosity was set aside when foreigners hired locals as guides. It was in everyone's interest to keep the tourists happy. And since she wasn't an archaeologist, she'd be considered a tourist. In other words, not a threat to business.

She gave a mental shrug. Maybe the heat was getting to her after all, and she really was imagining things. Why would he take her there if he thought he'd get into any real trouble for it? She wasn't naive enough to think he'd shown her every secret these cliffs were hiding. She just had to trust him enough to believe he would not let her down in her mission to find this one inscription.

And she did trust him. As far as it went.

She reined Dawar to follow the donkey along the skinny path at the foot of the *gebel*. After a few hundred yards they came to a stop. She looked up at the colorful sandstone crenulations of the cliffs, searching out the shadow he had spoken of.

"I don't see anything."

His eyes met hers, then quickly slid away. Unconsciously, he touched his amulet. "I must have been wrong." He *definitely* seemed nervous. "Come. Let's cont—"

"No, we may as well have a quick look around," she said, and dismounted. She'd never seen him like this before. Something was hidden around here, and she had every intention of finding out what. And why he seemed so jumpy.

After tying Dawar to a low bush she hiked the last few feet to the cliff, reaching out to touch its rough, sandy surface. Hot. Gritty. *No vibes.* She smiled in memory. Her mother, a true child of the sixties, had believed the earth held spirits you could hear and feel, if you only tried hard enough. It was important not to offend them or dishonor them. All three sisters still followed her habit of making a libation to the local spirits whenever they ate outside, and saying a prayer for safe passage through their lands. Better safe than sorry.

Unfortunately, no earth spirits spoke to Gillian today, either. She'd have to find whatever was hidden among the cliffs all on her own.

"But there is nothing," Mehmet protested, arms spread expansively. "Perhaps farther along—"

"What's that?" She squinted a few feet above her head. It was a shadow. Thin, but solid and black, clinging to a slight recess in the rock. She scrambled on all fours up the steep gravel alluvium to reach it.

"Miss!" Mehmet called after her. "Be careful! The sand is loose. It's dangero—"

"My God! Look!" She reached the recess and peered behind the outcropping that hid it. "It's an opening! Just like you thought."

Tall and narrow like the eye of a needle, it was nevertheless large enough for a person to sidle through. Into what—if anything—was anyone's guess. But she intended to find out.

She reached for the small but powerful flashlight hanging next to the knife sheath on her belt. "I'm going in."

"Miss! Wait!"

She could hear Mehmet clamber hurriedly after her. But she had already switched on the flashlight, steeled her nerves and slid through the opening.

She blinked as her eyes adjusted from dazzling sunlight to near-complete darkness. And realized she was standing in an antechamber. To a tomb. Ancient, by the look of it. Which was nothing unusual in itself. The cliffs were riddled with them. The foyer-size chamber, bare of objects and ornamentation, was simply four square walls chiseled out of the sandstone.

Uninscribed walls, their only adornment lines carved in the rock to make it look like fitted blocks.

Damn.

She sighed in disappointment.

Mehmet poked his head in through the opening. His eyes darted frantically around the empty room. Then his shoulders notched down and again he touched his amulet. He reached for her arm. "You see? It's nothing. We should go."

She couldn't help the feeling that he was desperately trying to draw her away from this place. *Again, why?*

"Just a sec," she said, shook off his hand and took two steps to the center of the chamber. Slowly she trailed the beam of her flashlight over the walls. Searching…for anything that would tell her why Mehmet was acting so strangely.

That's when she found it. A narrow slot cleverly carved between two faux blocks, so well-hidden that anyone who had not grown up trekking through tombs and temples with an

Egyptologist father would never have spotted it. Maybe not even then.

Her scalp prickled and a rash of goose bumps surged over her arms. She walked over to examine it closer. "What do we have here?"

"No! Miss, please. You shouldn't be here. Let us leave this place at once."

She turned to him. His mouth was twisted in fear. Good lord. These rivals must be ruthless.

"Mehmet, you know you can trust me," she tried to assure him. "Whatever else this tomb contains is none of my business. I am only interested in one thing—the Kilpatrick inscription. If it's here, I'll take pictures and we can leave. I swear I'll tell no one of its existence."

He shook his head vigorously. "You don't understand."

"Go get the camera from the saddlebag," she instructed crisply. "The sooner we find out if the inscription is here, the sooner we can go."

He stared at her for a moment, then turned jerkily and left, muttering something unintelligible under his breath.

Okay, then.

Drawing her knife from its sheath on her hip, she gingerly inserted the blade, probing for the trip-latch she hoped she'd find. The tomb must be Ptolemaic. Only during the Greek period did such devices exist, then rarely, and to her knowledge only in the temples. A priest was probably buried here. Odd, though, this far south. Most of the real Greeks had stayed up north in Lower Egypt.

There! The knife tip hit something metallic. Carefully she pushed down on it. A low rumble started in the bowels of the tomb, and slowly, a square section of the rock started to move backward. When it stopped, it revealed a hole large enough for a man to crawl through.

Good heavens.

She swallowed, the goose bumps on her arms tickling like mad. She rubbed her palms over them, then reached for the water bottle in her trouser cargo pocket. She poured a generous libation on the ground.

Then she sucked down a deep breath, dropped to her knees and crawled into the hole.

Chapter 3

So hurry to see your lady,
Like a stallion on the track…
                 —Later Period love song

"She is close. So close I can smell the sweet scent of her woman's blood."

Rhys turned to Seth and let his lips curve in a smile. "Indeed." Rhys could smell her, too. Not her blood, but a faint tracing of flowers and vanilla-scented skin. Lovely. Arousing. "What would you have me do with her, my lord? Frighten her away, or…?"

Seth paced across the malachite council-room floor, his tall warrior's frame erect, his face betraying no emotion that Rhys could discern. "She must not be allowed to find that inscription if it brings your curious descendents down upon us."

"I agree. That would be a disaster." They'd already had one too-close call back in the twenties, when that pompous American archaeologist nearly discovered their secret eastern entrance.

A soft rumbling reached the room from the far-off surface, more of a vibration in their minds than a real sound. They both glanced up in surprise.

"Good God. She's found the entrance," Rhys said, his stomach dropping. He'd arranged for the boy, one of his mortal familiars, to lead her to the hidden tomb, hoping the plain-rock antechamber would put an end to her curiosity. He'd never expected her to discover the secret way in.

"And by finding it, she has decided her fate," Seth said.

"Shall I set her capture in motion?" Rhys

asked cautiously. The alternative would not be a pleasant one for her. He would fight it, if it came to that.

"You've seen this woman?" Seth asked, clasping his hands behind his back. Meeting Rhys's eyes.

"From a distance," he granted. "She looked… dusty." Which was the truth, if not the whole of it. For some reason, dust and all, the woman intrigued Rhys. Even now he could feel the rhythm of his heart increase at the thought of her.

Seth's brows moved infinitesimally. "And she's a foreigner, you say."

"American, I believe. Tall, pale and blond. She was with two other women down at the ruined temple of Sekhmet. Sisters, my informant tells me."

The other man's black eyes glowed with obvious interest. "Hmm. A blonde to replace the *shabti* Haru-Re stole from me last month."

"Yes. Or she would make a fine initiate. She seems intelligent. Respectful." And had the right color hair. Which was why she'd attracted Rhys's attention in the first place, when he'd heard about the three beautiful foreign women. Seth was partial to blondes, and accessible ones were rare in this part of the world, off the beaten tourist path as they were. Especially in these days of random, violent terrorism.

Of course, now that she'd discovered Khepesh's secret entrance, there was little choice in the matter.

"True. I could use her for the Ritual of Transformation," Seth said thoughtfully. "And if I like her, take her as my consort. I miss having a helpmate at my side."

Rhys fought a scowl. *That* would change things. If Seth claimed her, the woman would be off-limits to Rhys, on pain of banishment, or even death. Not exactly what he'd had in mind. Being the demigod's master steward had many advantages. But it also involved an occasional bit of frustration. Rhys was also partial to blondes. At least this one.

"The transformation ceremony," he said, deliberately downplaying the consort idea. "Yes, why not. If Nephtys gives her blessing, of course."

The rumbling of the entrance stone ceased abruptly.

Seth looked up again. "But is it really wise to take her?" he asked with a frown that in no way disguised his desires in the matter. "Foreigners do bring a welcome change, but they are always such a risk. Especially if there's family who will miss them."

"Not an insurmountable difficulty," Rhys assured. There were ways of dealing with troublesome relatives, if necessary. As long as they were here in Egypt. "I believe she only has the two sisters. And they are easily bespelled." Young women were especially susceptible to... influence.

"Perhaps an accident would be more prudent."

"You did say to increase our number," Rhys argued reasonably, when what he really wanted to do was shout, *No! You will not harm her!* "And fresh blood for the ceremony would be a good thing for you."

"Yes." Seth's expression resolved. "Then go quickly, my friend. Assess the situation. Use your considerable charm to bring this woman willingly to our side. But if it turns into more trouble than she's worth, take care of her." His gaze pierced Rhys's. "We don't need any more problems right now."

"Yes, my lord." Rhys bowed his head, turned and strode from the room.

A thrum of excitement buzzed through him. For the past few days the woman had been wandering too close for comfort to their underground palace, so he had decided to arrange an encounter through his informant. The boy had been strangely reluctant to expose her, so Rhys had gone out earlier to subtly remind him of the consequences of failure.

The woman had spotted him as he'd gazed down on her in anticipation. Even from high atop the *gebel* he'd felt a charge of electricity from the way she'd returned his perusal.

Awed. Worshipful. Like she wanted to wrap her thighs around him and ride all day.

She would be no shabti, he thought determinedly.

She would make a fine prize for the god— and afterward, for himself. He would see to it that the ceremony did not damage her. As for becoming Seth's consort, well, he would simply have to find someone else for that.

This woman was *his*.

Black robes flying and boot heels clicking a determined tattoo on the hallway's marble floor, he quickly made his way through the Great Western Gate and the winding tunnels that led to a rock-hewn stairway and the world above. When he burst out from the well-concealed opening, high up on the *gebel* where no human would dare climb, he gathered his robes and spun in a swift circle, chanting the magical words of the spell that Nephtys had gifted him on the night of his transformation. The powerful words that would change his human flesh into his immortal form.

The stallion, al Fahl.

Having shifted to the beast within, he reared up and pawed the air in growing anticipation, then took off at a gallop, seeking the path that would take him to the woman. The woman he had chosen to bow before the altar of the Lord of Darkness. The woman destined, if all went well, to be Set-Sutehk's next blood sacrifice.

And his own newest conquest.

* * *

Gillian hesitated on her hands and knees just inside the inner tomb opening, unwelcome thoughts of vampires stealing through her mind. The interior room was blacker than midnight.

She swallowed. If she crawled in all the way, would the sandstone block slide home again, trapping her inside the hidden tomb? Her heart hammered so hard she feared it would slam right out of her chest. Surely, there would be a lever on this side, too....

Stifling a shiver, she raised her flashlight to look around before deciding. But her hands were shaking so badly she dropped the light. The clatter of hard plastic on stone echoed through the chamber, hinting at its size. Not huge, but a good deal larger than the antechamber.

"Mehmet?" she yelled over her shoulder. Where had the kid gotten to?

He didn't answer. Nor did she hear the comforting pad of torn sneakers on the stone floor behind her.

Turning back inside, she took a deep, cleansing breath of surprisingly fresh air. This was ridiculous. There were no such things as vampires. And she'd been in a thousand tombs before. This one was no different. Well. Except for the weird sliding stone. That was unusual. But certainly nothing to be all paranoid about.

She let out the breath, picked up her flashlight and shone it around.

An involuntary cry arose in her throat. "Sweet Mother of God!"

Shock and excitement surged up within her. Forgetting all about being trapped, she vaulted to her feet, wildly aiming the flashlight around the room.

It was amazing!

Beautiful, precisely chiseled inscriptions and breathtaking painted scenes covered the walls on all sides. Old Kingdom, if she didn't miss her mark. And truly incredible!

She swept the flashlight beam to the main funerary scene on the focal wall. Which showed clearly it was not a Ptolemaic priest's tomb at all, but a far more ancient priest who had served—she stepped closer, stilling the beam on the central figure of the scene—the god Set-Sutekh. The tall, distinctive figure of the half man, half mythical jackal-like creature stood regally in a pose he'd held for five thousand years, accepting gifts and adulation from the slightly smaller figure of a human priest-servant.

She squinted at the inscription alongside the man, dredging up the hieroglyphics she'd learned as a child, traipsing after her father and a bossy sister who liked to tease her with secret messages written in obscure glyphs. The priest's name was…Seth-Aziz.

Her eyes widened and she let out a nervous laugh. *Oh, shit.* The vampire? Seriously?

She forced herself to take a deep breath. "Get a grip, girl," she scolded herself. Seth-Aziz was not an uncommon name in those times. Presumably this one had been the builder of the tomb, and its original occupant. A priest. *Not* a vampire.

She concentrated on the funerary scene. Fanning off to either side of the deceased were other, even smaller figures of men and women, as well as gorgeous carvings of flowers, birds and animals. It was all simply stunning.

"Oh, man," she said softly, drowning in the beauty of the painting. There was something magical about it. Something almost…alive. Despite its age and the classic Egyptian stylization of the depictions, the figures seemed almost to…to breathe with vitality and life. Again, goose bumps whispered over her skin. "I hope you paid your artists well, Seth-Aziz, for they created something truly worthy of your god."

She savored the rest of the scene, taking it in slowly, bit by bit, sounding out the names of the other family members and followers depicted worshipping the great god Set-Sutekh, along with the High Priest Seth-Aziz. Some stood, some knelt respectfully on their heels. Some danced or played instruments. All were carefully named. Even the birds and animals had names.

"Mehmet!" she yelled again, aiming her flashlight at the crawl hole. "You have got to see this! Hurry! Where's that camera?"

As she turned back to the carved figures, a man toward the end of the line of Seth's human supplicants caught her attention.

He had a mustache.

"What the…?"

Egyptians didn't do mustaches. Ever. He must have been a captive. A foreigner who had somehow worked his way into the high priest's respect. Curious, she walked up and peered closely at the inscription running along his back. She didn't recognize any of the words. Or the name.

"Lard...Lerd Roos...Rees..." she sounded out aloud. One of the big annoyances with hieroglyphics was that, like Arabic, they didn't contain the vowels used for pronunciation, and unless you knew the word, you just had to guess. "Okay, definitely a foreign name. So, Lerd Roos or Rees, Khel... Khilpet...Khelpet Rech. Lard Roos Khelpetrech. Lord—"

She let out a gasp and dropped her flashlight again. This time the bulb popped, plunging the tomb into pitch darkness. But she barely noticed. Instead, she was frantically trying to tame her thoughts. The inscription had been clearly carved in the same style as the rest of the figures. Not graffiti.

Impossible!

That's when a stranger's voice suddenly came from behind her. "I see you've found me."

A man's voice.

Not Mehmet's.

With a scream, she whirled, instinctively flattening herself against the tomb wall, vainly searching the darkness. "Who's there?"

She reached for her knife. It wasn't in its sheath. She must have dropped it in the excitement of opening the secret door.

The scrape of boots sounded like he was moving through the crawl hole, then a soft rustle of fabric as he straightened. *Inside the tomb with her.* Panic crawled up her spine. This wasn't some mythical vampire. This was a real man. Possibly a tomb robber. *Or worse.* Why hadn't she listened to Mehmet?

"Don't be alarmed." The voice was calm and smooth, with a cultured British accent. Which didn't mean squat. Jack the Ripper's accent probably sounded sexy as hell.

The boots stepped closer. She pressed herself harder into the wall. But there was no escape through solid stone.

She wanted to squeeze her eyes shut but didn't dare. Though it hardly mattered. The darkness was so thick it wrapped around her like a black velvet blanket, heavy and cloying. She could barely breathe. She started to feel faint—and her knees were growing weak.

There was something wrong with her.

"Who are you?" she managed, fighting to stay upright.

The boots stopped right in front of her. Her stomach clenched wildly. She was so dead.

"My name is Lord Rhys Kilpatrick."

A strange, encompassing energy welled through her mind like a rising tide of buzzing insects. "Yeah, right," she muttered, shaking her head, desperately trying to clear it. But the motion only made it worse. "And I'm Amelia Edwards."

She was sure she heard a soft, masculine chuckle. But then she lost the battle with her knees and slowly started to slide down the block wall. *Oh, God.*

Her last thought was of her sisters. *Please don't let them take this too hard....*

Then she collapsed, right into the arms of the stranger.

Chapter 4

The fire is laid, the fire shines;
The incense is laid on the fire
Your perfume comes to me; May my
perfume come to you.
May I be with you; May you be with me.

—Pyramid Text 269

The priestess Nephtys rested her chin in her hands and her elbows on the well-worn rim of her favorite scrying basin, which she'd long ago named the Eye of Horus. Two hands deep and wide as the god's shoulders, the large round bowl had been fashioned in ancient times from a single piece of the finest golden amber and polished to satin smoothness. It carried a slight fragrance of ambergris. Thus it was pleasing to the senses as well as being unfailingly honest in the visions it produced. The Eye of Horus had yet to be wrong, regardless of how depressing or uncomfortable the glimpses it brought to Nephtys of the future. Or, indeed, of the present.

Wistfully, she gazed down into the sparkling clear water that rippled gently in the bowl as though the god himself blew softly across its surface.

Would she see him today? The man she loved. The man who had traded her away without a second thought... Because at the time she'd been a lowly slave, unworthy of the high priest's serious attentions. A quick sip of her blood, a thorough fucking, then instantly forgotten. A sensual curiosity, no more, mainly due to her snow-white skin and exotic head of wavy red hair, which he'd loved to spread across his fine linen pillow. But to her, even then he'd been every inch the demigod he was destined to become. Black-haired and black-eyed, he nevertheless had skin that glowed with the burnished gold of the sun he so faithfully served. His robes were woven in the hues of sunrise, glittering with strands of golden threads that shot through the fabric. He was truly worthy of awe, and as a captive in his household she had fallen in love with him the first moment she'd laid eyes on him. Still a virgin, she'd given herself to him more than willingly, always yearning for his touch, his glance, his regard. Never daring to hope for his heart, which she knew she would never possess. But she had not expected to be discarded quite so callously. Ceded to his greatest enemy without a backward glance.

And that, more than anything else, had spurred her ambition, compelling her to rise in station, to become the most powerful priestess in the land. And now, she was the only one who possessed the secret of shifting the flesh of man to beast.

Oh, how *that* must chagrin the heartless bastard! Certainly, it had caused his endless attempts over the centuries since to rectify his massive error in judgment by capturing her back. But her adopted brother, Seth, guarded her carefully, sparing no expense or effort in keeping her safely out of enemy hands.

Her brother was her greatest joy.

Since that crushing day so many years ago, she had rarely allowed herself to seek her former lover's image in the magic waters of her scrying bowl. Who needed the painful reminder of her maidenly folly? Even five millennia later, it still stung. And her heart still yearned for… that which her pride would never countenance.

Sometimes his image appeared in the waters of its own volition, giving her a glimpse into his life, usually more disturbing than helpful. But it had been ages now. Which was a good thing. For whenever his image appeared, trouble invariably followed. For her brother, Seth-Aziz, for Khepesh, but most of all for herself…and her foolish, foolish heart.

This morning as she gazed into the bowl, the water clouded and the ripples started to swirl. A vision was being formed. She sat up and paid close attention. Abruptly, the water cleared.

In its depths, she saw the rows of silver, papyrus-shaped columns of the inner temple.

Khepesh's holy of holies. A ceremony was taking place, and she recognized the extravagant trappings of the annual Ritual of Transformation. Seth-Aziz was there, of course, leading the proceedings. A woman stood before him. To her surprise, Nephtys saw that she was a foreigner, like herself, but younger and blond. She was dressed in the gorgeous, embroidered stole that marked her as belonging to the High Priest of Khepesh. Her eyes were heavily made-up, her lips the color of pomegranates.

The demigod's blood sacrifice.

The woman appeared singularly unhappy. And frightened out of her wits.

Then she looked up and her green eyes flared with hope—along with something that looked a lot like…love. And Seth returned her look of adoration.

Nephtys peered closer into the bowl, overjoyed. Finally, her brother would find a woman worthy of his love and devotion! Could this be the woman who would become Seth-Aziz's consort, destined to sit at his side for the rest of her existence, sharing her body with him, as well as her life's blood?

The vision abruptly cut to the future. Yes! The woman had become Seth's consort. The demigod and his bride—appearing somewhat older now without her elaborate makeup—were seated in raised chairs in the audience chamber, holding hands affectionately.

But the consort was speaking to a crowd of shouting, terrified followers. Something bad was about to befall the palace. Amazingly, when she spoke the people quieted and listened to her, and their agitation calmed visibly.

The high priest's future consort was obviously a very wise woman, destined to gain the respect of her husband's flock. Though what advice she was giving, and toward what end, only time would tell. The visions allowed Nephtys to see, but not to hear what was going on, so she could only guess at what was happening. But it looked grim for Khepesh. Such anxiety among the people could only mean one thing.

War.

Nephtys's stomach sank.

Seth-Aziz had but one enemy left. And that enemy had only one reason to wage war upon her brother.

Nephtys herself.

A shiver went through her, sending tingles of forbidden joy through her flesh. Secretly, in her heart of hearts, a bud of unwilling exhilaration unfurled.

Soon, Haru-Re, high priest to Re-Horakhti, Keeper of the Sun, Guardian of the Day, and betrayer of her own heart, would be here.

Her lover was coming for her again. And this time she feared—and prayed—he would succeed.

Rhys gathered the unconscious woman in his arms. He'd been debating whether he should carry her directly into the palace as a captive, as Seth had urged, or first make an attempt to convert her as a willing initiate of the god, as his own conscience dictated. Not to mention his lust.

On the one hand, time was short. But Rhys abhorred the idea of *shabti*s, as the human servants were called, who were as good as slaves.

And there was plenty to entice a woman to give herself over to the god and immortality by choice. Even in the early years when one was confined to the palace, despite its perpetual dimness of nighttime, life at Khepesh was filled with sensual delights and challenges for both mind and body. If not for the wretched threats of war with Haru-Re, it would truly be paradise on earth.

The delicate scent of the woman he carried wove around his senses, tugging at his nether regions. It had been too long since he'd been with a woman. His duties had kept him too busy of late. Standing here in the dark, the soft and vulnerable feminine flesh laid out across his arms was a vivid reminder of what he'd been missing. Soon, he hoped, the situation would be remedied.

Unless Seth decided to keep her beyond the Ritual of Transformation ceremony. Rhys just hoped he'd be able to keep his hands off her long enough to talk Seth into gifting her to him. The ceremony was less than a week away. He could hold out until then.

Cradling her head against his shoulder to

protect her from scraping against the stone walls, he held her body close to his and ducked out through the tomb opening, blinking back the blinding sunlight as he slid through the needle's eye in the rock cliff. And was greeted by a sharp shout from below.

"Hey! What are you doing with her?"

A very angry woman rushed up at him, rocks and gravel flying as she scrambled. A second woman took a stance stock-still at the bottom of the slope…aiming a rifle at his head.

"Put her down!" the woman holding the rifle ordered him with cold fierceness. Apparently, she was very sure of her aim. If Rhys hadn't known he could easily deflect her earthly bullets, he might actually be worried.

"You must be the sisters," he called, readjusting the woman's weight in his arms. She moaned and turned her cheek against his throat, sliding her own arm around his neck to cling to him. The intimate gesture made the sisters' eyes widen. The one coming at him with raised fists halted in her tracks, staring, giving him exactly the opportunity he needed.

He gathered his immortal powers and sent

out a wave of forgetfulness to engulf them both. Not enough to render them unconscious, as he had the woman while in the tomb, but enough to blank their minds and open them to his control. Slowly the fists and rifle dropped harmlessly to their sides.

"You will forget you ever saw me here, or your sister," he commanded. "When we are gone, you will proceed as though this meeting never happened."

They stood like statues, their eyes unseeing, hanging on his every word.

"When she contacts you, you will believe I am not a danger. You will not be alarmed, nor take any action to stop her when she says she intends to stay with me. Is that understood?"

"Yes," they both chanted softly.

Satisfied they would obey, he effortlessly swung the woman around onto his back, twining her arms securely about his neck. With a whirl of his cloak and a swirling of sand in the air, he again recited the magic words that would transform him to al Fahl.

Then, securing his precious cargo on his back with a tethering spell, he reared up and took off at a fast gallop. He'd made up his mind. He would take her to his desert estate.

And there he would work a different kind of magic on her….

Gillian slowly became aware of lying on something silky and sumptuous and very large. A bed? Certainly not her own narrow bed back at the villa she and her sisters were renting for the season. She stirred, feeling cool satin sheets slide beneath her body. And realized her shirt and boots had been removed, leaving her barefoot, wearing just her trousers and a cotton camisole.

Where was she?

And what on earth had happened to her?

"Ah, you're back with me at last," a deep, masculine voice murmured from the undulating brink of consciousness.

Her eyes fluttered open.

A man sat on the bed, looking down at her.

Tall and muscular, he had black hair and a striking black mustache in an arrestingly handsome face. But it was his eyes that really commanded her attention. Piercing, amber eyes ringed with black and flecked with gold, they watched her with calm, deadly concentration. *The gaze of a predator observing his prey...*

A tremble sifted through her whole body. It was...*him*. The man from the tomb. She knew it down to her still-shaking knees. She wanted to tear her gaze away from those mesmerizing eyes. But couldn't. Couldn't, because along with being terrifying, she also found the dark stranger...incredibly attractive.

"Where am I?" she managed, unable to stop herself from surreptitiously brushing her throat with her fingers, foolishly checking for bites.

He smiled, revealing a hint of straight white teeth. "My estate. You fainted in the tomb. Lucky I was there to catch you," he said in his cultured British accent.

She swallowed, positive it was *because* he'd been there that she'd fainted. *If* that's what had happened. She had the oddest feeling that he'd somehow deliberately caused her blackout. Though she couldn't imagine how.

"Yes, lucky," she said, closing her eyes against a shiver. *He'd caught her in his arms.* Touched her. And carried her off to his house.

An involuntary frisson zinged through her insides as she suddenly remembered her lack of a shirt. God knew what else he'd done.…

"Shall I call a doctor to make sure you're okay?" he asked, interrupting her alarming thoughts.

"No." Gillian sat up. "I'm fine. Really. A few sips of water, and—"

"You're very warm. It might be sunstroke," he warned. "We should try to bring down your body temperature."

Too bad the way he was looking at her had the opposite effect. Which, under the circumstances, was pure insanity.

"Sunstroke? Inside a tomb?"

He ignored her pointed comment. "Perhaps you'd like to take a cooling bath?" he suggested.

She blinked, her nervousness shifting into a completely different sort. Her heartbeat kicked up. "I really don't think—"

Rising, he indicated a door next to a lavish built-in wardrobe. "You should find everything you need in the bathroom, through here. I'll send someone with a change of clothes for you." He turned to leave the room.

"Wait," she said. Had she been wrong about him? She could have sworn she'd seen something hidden, something…dangerous…in the stranger's eyes. Or was she imagining it all? "You never told me who you are."

His smile did a mysterious curl at the corner of his lips. "You don't remember?"

She tried to dredge her mind, but it was like peering through layers of fog. "Sorry, no. I'm Gillian Haliday, by the way," she added, her pulse pounding.

"Gillian. What a lovely name. Very nice to meet you, Miss Haliday. I'm Rhys. Rhys Kilpatrick."

She literally felt the blood drain from her face as the fog dissolved and a flash of disturbing memories came flooding back. Of their meeting in the tomb.

Oh, God.

The bizarre inscription. The voice in the darkness. *His* voice.

The voice of a dead man.

Chapter 5

My heart remembers how I once loved you,
As I sit with my hair half done,
And then I'm out looking for you,
Searching for you with my hair half done!
    —Song of the Birdcatcher's Daughter

"Who are you really?"

Indeed. How much to tell her?

Before answering Gillian's curt demand, Rhys finished uncorking a bottle of chilled Pouilly-Fuissé and poured them each a generous portion in his best crystal goblets. Then he turned to his houseguest. She stood under the onion-domed archway to the salon, regarding him suspiciously. He had long since shed his keffiyeh and *agal,* and his black outer cloak, but was still wearing the traditional black riding pants and tunic favored by the Bedouin. A somewhat sinister look, judging by the hint of fear lurking in her eyes.

Moments ago she'd slammed and locked the bedroom door after him, that same fear shading her whole face because he'd allowed her to remember. But now her expression had turned determined, if a little uneasy. Brave woman. He was impressed.

Her ivory skin was still damp from splashing water on her face and neck in the sink. She hadn't trusted him enough to take the recommended bath. Not that he blamed her.

Wisps of blond hair curled in wet ringlets around her temples, and her large, troubled green eyes peered at him from a face that was lovely despite its lack of makeup. A coil of desire wound through his body.

"Wine?" he offered, noting with displeasure that she was not wearing the dress he'd had his housekeeper lay out for her. Of the finest faience-blue silk, he'd chosen it especially to complement her delicate coloring. And her attractive curves.

On the plus side, her thin camisole stretched quite pleasingly over her full breasts. A fair compensation.

She took a step forward, hesitation in the movement. "Please, just answer the question."

"I told you. I'm Rhys Kilpatrick."

"Lieutenant Rhys Kilpatrick died a hundred twenty-five years ago."

"Yes, he did," he agreed, somewhat truthfully.

"Well, then?"

He met her accusing gaze. Briefly considered bespelling her again to avoid her questions. Discarded the idea. No, he'd have to do this the old-fashioned way.

Well. Mostly.

"What exactly are you accusing me of being?" He chuckled. "A ghost, or…a vampire, perhaps?" He glanced meaningfully through the windows at the blazing sun.

Her cheeks flushed. "How about a con man?"

He hiked a brow. "You think I'm lying? To what end?" he asked, curious as to her train of thought.

"How about a fortune? Playing the long-lost relative to a wealthy English viscount could prove very lucrative to someone smart enough to pull it off."

He pursed his lips, again impressed. She was dead wrong, but it was a very intelligent guess, nonetheless. "Believe me," he said drily, "the last thing I want is for the Kilpatrick family to learn of my existence. I must insist you swear you'll never mention me to anyone even remotely connected with them. In fact, anyone at all."

That drove her into a moment's silence. "Why?" she finally asked, reluctantly accepting the glass of wine from him.

"Unnecessary complications. I like my life here in Egypt and would deeply resent any attempt to alter it. Which would inevitably happen if the truth came out."

"What truth?"

"That I am living proof Rhys Kilpatrick did not die as reported."

"I see."

No, she didn't. But she would soon enough.

"Are you his direct descendent?" she asked, her mistrust fading to fascinated speculation.

"As direct as it gets," he said.

She took a thoughtful sip of wine, momentarily distracting him with the shape of her lips. Elegantly curved, lushly plump. Lips made for—

"So, they are all valid, then."

He jerked his gaze up. "What's that?"

"The rumors the family wants to disprove. About the lieutenant's desertion from the army. That he had joined some kind of bizarre Egyptian cult and—" Suddenly she gasped, her eyes going wide. "Oh, my God. The tomb inscription! *That's* what it was all about!"

Good lord. A direct hit. Beautiful, alluring and smart as Isis. There was no way he could let her go now, even if he wanted to. Which he was feeling less and less inclined to do in any case.

"I'm afraid you are correct," he allowed. "Although it's not called a cult here. The proper term is *per netjer,* which means 'house of the god.' 'Cult' sounds so…sinister."

"You mean they're *not?* Wow." Her mouth opened then closed again. Fear was creeping back onto her face. "But surely, *you* aren't—"

He winked. "Worried I intend to carry you off to some secret underground temple and sacrifice your innocence to Set-Sutekh?"

She blinked. "Don't be silly. I'm serious."

"Oh, so am I. Perfectly."

Her laugh at his mock solemnity crackled with nervousness, so he took pity on her and smiled. "Do I really look so dangerous and disreputable, Miss Haliday?"

Her gaze lowered and skittered away. "Possibly."

The odd thing was, he got the unexpected feeling she'd meant the assertion more as a compliment than an insult.

As though she, too, realized it, she suddenly developed an interest in the decor, taking in his sumptuous furniture, the luxurious throws and pillows, the fragrant flowers and flickering candles scattered about the room, the artwork and antiquities gracing the walls and shelves.

"You have a beautiful home, Lord Kilpatrick."

"Rhys," he said. "Call me Rhys. Thank you." After the austere, almost severe settings of his childhood, he loved surrounding himself with sensual objects. It was one of the things that had drawn him to his new life in the first place.

"How long have you lived here?"

He drained his wine and refilled it, then strolled over to top hers up, as well. "Seems like I've owned the estate forever. But I split my time between here and another residence, a bit farther south."

She picked up a framed daguerreotype of him and the famous archaeologist Flinders Petrie, taken at the ruins of the temple of Seth in Naqada during the excavations of 1895. The old boy had been an odd duck, but interesting. Rhys had still been in his exploratory phase back then, traveling the country as a spy for Shahin, soaking up the culture, blending in with the steady stream of aristocratic Victorian tourists doing the grand tour. He'd met some fascinating people and learned a hell of a lot. Exciting times.

She squinted at the faded sepia photo. "I

don't believe it. That's Flinders Petrie! Standing with—" She looked up in amazement. "This must be the original Rhys Kilpatrick!"

He nodded. "Indeed."

"But—but that's incredible! This must have been taken ten years after his supposed death. Do you have any idea how valuable this photo would be to the Kilpatrick family?"

He wagged a finger. "Don't even think about it. Remember, you swore to keep my existence a secret."

She tipped her head, taking his measure for a long moment. "It appears I may have misjudged you."

She had no idea.

He eased the photograph from her fingers and set it back on the mantel. "I'm glad you've decided to trust me." Unable to resist touching her, he brushed a damp curl from her cheek. "Honestly, I mean you no harm, nor the Kilpatricks."

He sensed the fine pulse in her neck pick up speed. Because he was near, practically bending over her? A spurt of hot pleasure shot through his blood at the thought that he attracted her as much as she attracted him.

Her lips parted a fraction. "That's good," she said, almost a whisper. "Um, do you have any more?"

It took a second for her question to push past the sudden desire to lean down and taste those tempting lips. "More what?" *Lust?*

"Old photographs. Of the original Lord Kilpatrick. And your other family members. Father, mother. I'm a historian, you see, and I'd love to—"

"Yes. Yes, of course," he interrupted, turning away abruptly. *He must control himself.* There'd be an eternity to enjoy such pleasures later on, after she'd accepted her destiny and joined the immortals of Set-Sutekh. "Come, we'll open another bottle of wine in my study, and you can look through my photo albums."

She wouldn't miss noticing that the man in all the pictures looked exactly like him. *Was* him. Convincing her to come with him to Khepesh would be that much easier if she'd already seen evidence of his unnatural longevity. Seeing was believing.

He quickly instructed his houseman to fetch another bottle of chilled wine, along with some cheese and fruit, and ushered Gillian down a long hallway to his favorite room in the house.

His study was dark and masculine, smelling of old books and leather furniture, mingled with the sweet spice of cut flowers that always filled an alabaster vase on his desk. Outside double French doors behind the desk was the *riad-*style home's enclosed central patio. Because of the skill of his Moroccan architect in angling walls, archways and an overarching pergola to produce ample shade, even on the hottest days Rhys could keep the French doors open and enjoy a cool breeze. Not to mention the lush, sensual colors and earthy scents of the carefully cultivated courtyard garden. Living in the semidarkness of Khepesh made him extra appreciative of the bounties of the sun. Though he'd never shift his allegiance, ever.

Maybe that was why he was so drawn to Gillian, with her exotic golden hair and pale skin. Because she was so different from himself and the dark world he lived in.

Not that he was complaining. Not in a million years. He loved the sensuous, mysterious, dark world of Khepesh, and would not trade it for anything in the universe. Certainly he enjoyed his regular forays up into the light, but he was not blinded by it. The underworld was his true home now. For all time.

Gillian curled up on his soft leather divan and eagerly looked through the old photo album he pulled from behind the leaded-glass doors of a bookcase as old as he. Gingerly, she turned the pages one by one, examining the photos with growing excitement.

"This is incredible," she murmured over and over as she sipped her wine and nibbled on grapes, studying the evidence of his long, exhilarating life in his beloved adopted country. "Lieutenant Kilpatrick seems to have met everyone who was anyone in those days. Not just Egyptologists, but politicians, writers, even the early movie stars."

Rhys pulled out the rest of the albums and handed her another one, then topped up her wine up once more. "Back then there weren't nearly as many foreigners in Egypt. It was pretty much expected that anyone living here would show visiting countrymen the local sights and invite them to dine."

She looked up. "But the lieutenant had deserted the army, and was supposed to be dead. How did he get away with that?"

He propped a shoulder against the bookcase and crossed one ankle over the other. "By using an assumed name."

"Ah." She nodded, leafing through more pages. "That makes sense." A small frown worked itself across her forehead.

"But…?" he asked, knowing full well what was beginning to bother her.

She shook her head. "It's just strange."

He strolled over to stand in front of her. "What is?"

She slanted her gaze up at him again. "The years are obviously going by in the photos, fashions are changing, hairstyles, the automobiles in the pictures. But…your predecessor doesn't seem to be aging at all."

"Mmm." He slid onto the couch next to her and took the album from her hand.

"You know, *you* look like him, too," she said,

examining his face, feature by feature, with growing disquiet. "*Exactly* like him."

"So I look like I'm a hundred twenty-five years old, eh?" he asked, an amused curve to his lips.

"Oh! No, I didn't mean—"

"You, on the other hand," he said, tossing the albums onto the stack on the coffee table and leaning toward her, "don't look a day over twenty."

She sucked in a breath of surprise.

Her rounded lips were soft and pink, her cheeks rosy with a flush that ripped across them. *Too much to resist.*

Before he thought about what he was doing, he caught her chin in his fingers, closed the scant distance between them and covered her open mouth with his.

He touched his tongue to hers. Instantly, the taste of her surged through his senses. And just as instantly he was hard and thick as a temple column. With a groan of need, he wrapped his hand around her jaw and deepened the kiss, unleashing his sexual powers upon her.

He wanted her. He wanted her *now*.

She gasped as he deliberately wrapped her in his sensual aura, heating her blood, heightening her body's sensitivity, caressing her insides with invisible tendrils of pleasure.

She shivered and moaned, and he pushed her back on the divan, sliding his hand up her body, stroking his tongue into her mouth. Wanting to pour his desire into her like a drugging wine. To make her surrender. To claim her. To bind her to him and make her his own for all eter—

By the gods.

No!

He halted. What was he thinking? He could *not* do this. Not yet. There were things to be settled first. Not the least of which was whether Seth would claim Gillian for himself.

Rhys jerked back, tormented by the thought. He leaped to his feet, knocking the stack of albums on the table pell-mell to the floor in a snowstorm of sepia, black-and-white and Technicolor squares.

She gaped up at him from the divan, her breasts rising and falling with roughened breath, her nipples tight and pointed, her face flagged with embarrassment and confusion. "Wh-what's going on…?"

For the first time ever, jealousy roared through him. At his friend. At the fact that Seth was also his lord and his leader, and had the power to take whatever and whomever he wanted, and there was nothing Rhys could do about it.

"I—I'm sorry," he stammered, gathering himself. Tamping down the anger and the frustration. "My behavior was unforgivable." He backed away from her, knocking even more photos onto the plush Oriental rug.

"But…" Looking dazed and still hopelessly aroused, she sat up and raked her fingers through her long hair, shaking her head. "I don't underst—"

Suddenly, she froze, giving a strangled gasp. A loose photo teetered on the edge of the coffee table. She grabbed it before he could see much more than that it was fairly recent, showing a group of people gathered here at his estate, in the courtyard, for some kind of party. As she stared at it, her eyes inexplicably filled with tears.

He frowned in surprise. "Gillian, what is it?"

A soft sob came from her throat. The photo trembled in her grip. "Oh, Rhys. The woman in this picture."

"What? Who is she, darling?"

"She's my mother!"

Chapter 6

But your embraces alone give life to my
heart;
May Amun give me what I have found for
all eternity.

—Papryus Harris 500, song 12

"Surely, you're mistaken," Rhys said.

But he was wrong. "You think I don't recognize my own mother?" Gillian whispered.

She wiped her eyes and ran an unsteady finger over the dear face in the photo. Her mother looked so…young. In her memories, Gillian was ever the small child, and Isobelle Haliday was tall and smiling and beautiful. Gillian had always looked up to her and run to her when she'd needed a safe pair of loving, adult arms. Until they'd disappeared forever...

"Let me see," Rhys demanded with a frown.

Gillian handed him the photo and pointed to the auburn-haired woman sitting on an iron bench next to an attractive Egyptian man. She didn't look happy. Or unhappy. Her expression was strangely blank. Which was exactly how Rhys's looked as he peered closer at the picture.

"Do you know that man?" she asked. "The one sitting next to her?"

He cleared his throat. "Unfortunately, yes. He was not a good person."

Alarm sang through Gillian. Could this be the one who'd caused her mother to vanish all those years ago? A killer, or human trafficker? "Who is he? I must tell the police. Maybe they can—"

"The man is dead, Gillian," Rhys interrupted. "He died shortly after this photo was taken."

"Oh!" Her whole body sagged with bitter

disappointment. She let out a long, slow breath. "Damn. I had hoped…"

The very hardest thing about her mother's death was that they'd never found her body. For years Gillian and her sisters had hoped and prayed she would come back, alive and well. With amnesia. Or some heroic story of escape from evil slave traders. Or even a bad excuse. Any excuse. They'd just wanted her to finally come back to them. Her father had hunted everywhere, tracked down every possible lead. Presumably the police had, too. But no trace of her had ever been found. After ten years, she'd been pronounced dead.

"What happened to the man?" Gillian persisted.

Rhys handed the photo back to her. "He was killed in a fight."

She straightened. A *fight?* "Could the fight have had something to do with my mother? Maybe the people who killed him also—" She swallowed, unable to say the words.

"I very much doubt it," Rhys said soothingly.

"Still, the police should follow up," she insisted. "When did it happen?"

"A few weeks after the party. Flip it over. There should be a date."

She turned over the photo and read the date. Frustrated, she shook her head. "No. It says 1992."

"That sounds about right."

"But…" Her heart suddenly seized in her chest. "It can't be."

He frowned. "Why not?"

"Rhys, she disappeared in 1990."

His black eyes shot to hers, then back to the photo. His mouth thinned. As though…

My God. *He knew something!*

He did! She felt it as she saw the tension that swept over his body. The way he glared at the photo, hatred flaring in those expressive, all-seeing eyes.

"What is it?" she asked, jumping to her feet. She dug her fingers desperately into the fabric of his tunic. "Tell me, please!"

"Darling, calm yourself. I don't *know* anything."

For a fleeting instant her mind snagged on

the endearment. It was the second time he'd called her *darling* since their explosive and unexpected kiss—which he'd ended like a man who'd caught himself tonguing a serpent. A situation hardly meriting endearments between them.

She shook off the contradiction and focused on her mother. "But you suspect something."

He gently pried her fingers from his shirt, holding them between his strong hands. "It was a long time ago, Gillian. I may be way off track."

"Please, Rhys." Her voice cracked with the plea. "If there's any chance at all…any light you can shed on what happened to her, you've got to tell me, and go to the police."

He put his hands on her shoulders. "If you want real answers, going to the authorities is the last thing you should do," he informed her. "Anyway," he said with a kiss to her forehead, "it's probably just the wrong date written on the photo."

He slipped his arms around her and she allowed herself to be pulled into the uneasy comfort of his embrace. Her eyes welled up again as she looked through the French doors onto the patio where her mother had once sat and enjoyed this very man's hospitality.

Except...*the date*...

She glanced down at the photo again, which he'd set on the coffee table. Sure enough, Rhys was smiling into the camera, his arm around a beautiful flaxen-haired woman who was laughing up at him. Gillian ignored a spurt of jealousy at their intimacy, and forced herself to look closer at the "Rhys" in the photo. He didn't appear a minute younger than he did now. Which was a physical impossibility. The man embracing her today would have been a teenager the year the photo was supposedly taken. Was it Rhys's father? In which case—

Hope flared anew.

"It must have been your parents' party," she said. "Maybe they remember—"

"My parents are dead," he cut in.

Sympathy tempered her disappointment. "Oh, I'm sorry."

He released her and stepped away. "Don't be. It was a long time ago." He lifted a shoulder. "We never really got along anyway."

There was that chill in his voice again. She suspected there was a lot more to the story, but no way was she going to pry. Or ask why he had no interest in meeting his long-lost aristocratic family in England to make up for whatever bad blood ran through his relationship with his parents. There might be aunts and uncles, or cousins.

"Mine did," she said wistfully. "Got along, that is. My whole family. It about killed my father when my mother disappeared. He was never the same. He pretended to throw himself into his scientific research, but he really spent the rest of his life searching for her here in Egypt. My sisters and I got closer because he was so…absent. In the end he took his own life." She sighed.

"I'm so sorry," Rhys said. His voice was now warm and soothing. He took another pace away from her. "There may be another way to find out something." He sounded oddly reluctant to continue.

"Yes? What?" she prodded. Hope sparked in her heart.

"More like *who*. And you're not going to like it." He turned to regard her.

She pressed her fingers to her mouth. "If this person helps me find my mother, I'll worship the ground they walk on. My sisters will, too."

He gave her an odd smile. "That's more accurate than you think. The thing is, the person I'm thinking of is a seer. A priestess in the service of the *per netjer* of Set-Sutekh."

She blinked. Set-Sutekh? The ancient god? Something tickled her memory, just out of reach. "A *seer?* You mean—" She suddenly recalled the tomb inscriptions of Seth-Aziz and the god he served. *Set-Sutekh.* Good lord, were the rumors that the cult still existed *true?*

"Yes, Nephtys has very special abilities. She can see things in the past as well as the future. She is rarely wrong. She may be able to discern what happened to your mother, why she was with this man."

Logic and reason warred within Gillian against the irrational wish that what he was saying could be possible. But it wasn't. To think so would really be grasping at straws. Her hope vanished in a fit of logic, as quickly as it had sprung up. "I appreciate the thought," she told him with another sigh. "But I don't think so."

He nodded. "I understand. Most westerners find it difficult to believe in such things. If you change your mind, let me know. In the meantime, I'll see what I can find out through normal channels. But don't get your hopes up. It really would take a miracle. Still, this is Egypt, and stranger things have happened. I'll do my best."

For some reason she believed him. And also felt instinctively that if anyone had the power to solve the mystery of her mother's death once and for all, it was this incredible man.

She couldn't help the smile that spread within her. He'd rescued her from a dead faint in the tomb, and now he'd offered to fix the worst anguish of her entire life. Her mysterious stranger was a true hero.

A lock of raven-black hair fell over the thick lashes of his sensuous bedroom eyes as he captured her gaze.

He was also sexy as hell.

The memory of his kiss washed over her,

vivid, toe-curlingly arousing, drenching her with the desire to taste his lips again.

She took a deep breath. Didn't a hero deserve a hero's reward?

She took a step toward him. And another. He stood his ground, not moving, letting her come to him.

But his glittering eyes beckoned, urging her closer with an almost physical pull. The sensation intensified, brushing over the bare skin of her arms and shoulders, and lower, tingling over her chest and the exposed slopes of her breasts, making her shiver as though he really were touching her.

Suddenly, it wasn't danger she felt emanating from him. It was pure, feral temptation. The powerful, chaotic draw of this enigmatic stranger was all but impossible to resist.

She swallowed, feeling deliciously dizzy and light-headed, as if she were tipsy. Oh, how she wanted to drown in the feeling, to float in the sensation of being kissed and caressed by the otherworldly energy flowing hotly over her skin! *His* energy.

Her nipples spiraled hard, thrusting themselves against the thin, confining fabric of her camisole. She wanted it gone, to be naked to enjoy the rush of erotic sensations without interference.

"Take it off," he ordered softly, as though she'd spoken her wicked thoughts aloud.

What was happening to her? It was like the man had some kind of magical power over her. Over her will and her body.

But she didn't care.

She pulled the camisole over her head and tossed it aside. Lowering her arms she watched his eyes darken to brown velvet, taking in the sight of her naked breasts.

She wanted him to kiss and caress her. Slide his hands over the curve of her hips. Brush his lips along the swell of her breasts. Probe the moist, secret place between her thighs.

"Come to me," he said.

She felt the impact of his roughly spoken command cascade through her body, from the roots of her hair clear to her toes. Illicit excitement danced through her veins.

She closed the distance, coming next to him. She wanted him to pull her into his arms. She ached for his touch with a longing that took her breath away.

He reached out and undid the waist button of her cargo pants with a firm flick of his thumb. Then started to pull down the zipper. His eyes held hers, daring her to deny him.

She didn't.

He slid the trousers over her hips, and then her panties. Dipped his chin so she'd step out of them. And then she was completely naked. She shivered with anticipation.

Never before had she wanted a man like this. This badly. This thoroughly. Willing to do anything he wanted, if only he'd take her. Fill her. Use his hard, powerful body to make her shatter in a million pieces.

"You are perfection," he murmured, taking her in. "A goddess."

But still he did not touch her.

"I want you," she whispered shakily, stepping against him. Shivering at the male roughness of his tunic and the musky, masculine smell that filled her senses.

"I mustn't," he said, and her heart sank. "Not yet."

"But…why?" She put her hand to his chest, felt the firm, defined muscles under his clothes. "Why bare my body if you don't intend to use it?"

"There are things you don't know. About me. About…"

"About what?"

His steady gaze held hers for a long moment. "Me."

"I don't care," she admitted, weak with desire. She nestled against him. Brazen. Shameless. "Whatever it is, it doesn't matter."

And in that moment she truly believed it didn't.

His hands finally found her, glided slowly down her nude torso, grasped her hips and pulled her flush against him. His arousal, thick and long, strained at her belly through the folds of his Bedouin pants.

He *did* want her.

He wound his hand in her hair and tugged back her head, exposing the column of her throat to the brush of his lips. He kept tugging as he put his mouth to her skin and licked wetly down, down, bending her spine over his free arm in an arch so her breasts were offered up to him in a sacrifice of hot, tingling flesh.

His lips closed over a nipple and he suckled hard, sending a stunning shock wave of pleasure and pain straight to her core. She cried out. Craving more. *More.* He switched to the other and she nearly came.

Her knees buckled and he caught her up. She surrendered herself to him with a moan.

"I can't," he said, his voice raw with some intense inner conflict, even as he swept her onto an armless settee and laid her down on it.

"Please," she begged. Beside herself.

She groped at his clothes, trying to peel them away. To expose him to her as she was exposed to him. He evaded her efforts, instead grasping her knees and wrenching them apart.

She gasped. Utterly open. Vulnerable. Shivering with the desire to be taken by a man she'd met only an hour before. She didn't care. She wanted this.

He dropped down between her legs. Her heart thundered. He slid his hands along the backs of her thighs, raising them, spreading her. She shook with sudden terror, and with lush expectation, quivering under his hands, waiting breathlessly. Until finally, finally, he put his tongue to her, his lips, his mouth. To her sizzling need.

At his first fleeting touch, pleasure roared through her. She screamed at the tumultuous onslaught. And came apart under him.

It was the last thing she remembered.

Chapter 7

May your knives not get hold of me;
may I not fall into your shambles, for I
know your names.
I am one of those who follow the Master.

—*The Papyrus of Ani*

Rhys pleasured his woman until well after her moans of ecstasy faded and her body ceased to tremble and quake. He didn't want to stop. Not ever. Definitely not until he'd rammed himself into her, pounded mercilessly between her thighs and slaked the ravenous need that was eating at him from the inside out.

The swollen staff between his legs was worthy of Min, the outrageously endowed lord of fertility. And Rhys's willpower was flagging badly. Thank the gods he'd had the presence of mind to rob her of consciousness at her last quiver. So she couldn't demand he mount and ride her.

And she would have. For Gillian Haliday had well and truly succumbed to his will, and hungered for his dominion.

Which would have been a heady, powerful feeling, were she his to conquer. But her availability had yet to be determined. It was up to Seth who could have her. He dared not take what had not been granted. Even going as far as he'd done could cost him dearly.

He drew in a deep breath of her, savoring the bouquet of her wild passion and her desire for him. Again he had to fiercely battle back his own voracious craving.

He would have her. Soon.

Somehow, he would have her, he *must* have her. Regardless of Seth's capricious wishes.

He rose, carried her into the bedroom and draped her gently across the bed, next to the silk dress that had been laid out for her. As much as it pained him, after a brief inner struggle he pulled the dress over her head and covered her smooth, luscious body so he would not be further tempted.

Leaving her, he strode to the salon to pour himself a stiff drink. He needed to collect himself. Gather his wits. Renew his loyalties to his leader and his cause.

He'd just thrown back a second shot when there came a loud, insistent rapping on the front door of the villa.

"Kilpatrick! Open up!"

His blood froze and the hair on his neck stood at attention.

What in the name of Anubis was *he* doing here?

For it was none other than Khepesh's immortal enemy.

Haru-Re.

"Lord Haru-Re," Rhys greeted the man whom his houseman, Amr, ushered into the salon with scowling mistrust. "To what do I owe this...visit?"

He'd kept the man waiting while he'd closed the door to the bedroom. Under no circumstances did he want the bastard to see Gillian. Haru-Re would contrive to steal her from him simply for sport. And there would be no ritual ceremony involved. She would not survive *his* bite.

"Just in the area," his archenemy said casually. "Thought I'd pop in and see how you fare."

Right. The last time had been several years ago. Ray did not make house calls. He wanted something.

All smiles and affability, Ray appeared for all the world an everyday wealthy Middle Easterner calling on a friend. Except of course, Rhys's remote estate was situated deep in a shady valley on the mostly uninhabited West Bank specifically to discourage anyone "popping in." And the treacherous demigod was anything but a friend.

"I do not like being kept waiting," Haru-Re added with imperious acerbity.

He wore an expensive Western linen suit—white, of course—and a Panama hat, which he handed to Amr along with a falcon-headed walking stick. A bit much, Rhys thought, but he did cut quite the dashing figure. For a murdering thief.

Still, Rhys dared not insult the man. "Do forgive. Please join me," he invited. Enemy or no, there was a certain etiquette to interacting with the immortals of other cults—especially a high priest. A demigod's powers were infinitely greater than Rhys's. He didn't relish having his blood drained. "Drink?"

"I'd kill for a martini. Extra dry."

"I'm sure you would," Rhys agreed genially, signaling Amr to fetch a bottle of gin from the drinks cabinet while he filled a cocktail shaker with ice.

Haru-Re glanced around the empty room. "I heard you have company."

"Did you, now," Rhys said, adding a touch of vermouth, wishing it were poison. Except, of course, poison had little effect on vampires. An upset stomach, perhaps. Alas, death required far stronger means. Still, it would be gratifying to see Haru-Re puke his guts out.

"Where is she, then?" his guest asked.

Rhys poured and handed him his drink. "Who would that be?"

"The mortal I sense within these walls." Ray's lips curved knowingly. "The woman who perfumes your skin."

"None of your damned business," Rhys said pleasantly.

Haru-Re let out a bark of laughter. "You are brave, Englishman, I'll give you that."

"Are you by any chance threatening me?"

"Good God, no." Ray grinned affably.

"Then what exactly do you want?" Rhys asked, his voice betraying the slightest edge of annoyance at the untimely and unwelcome visit.

"To defeat your master and rule all of Egypt for the glory of Re-Horakhti, God of the Sun and Lord of the Sky." Haru-Re lifted his glass in a toast and drank half the martini down in a single swallow, then popped the olive into his mouth with a brilliant smile.

The audacity of the man was colossal.

"Yes, well, good luck wi[...] returning the toast. "*Darkne[...] state of things, not light. In the [...] else in the universe, there will still [...] Your puny sun is a mere candle in th[...] of space."

"How comforting on a cold night," Ha[...] said sardonically. "Myself, I prefer the wa[...] of day." He turned to the enclosed courtya[...] indicating the pots overflowing with flowers[...] "I see you also enjoy the blessings of the Lord of Dawn." He took a step closer, peering at a small plant bearing a crown of white blossoms, the essence of which had a powerful anesthetic effect on anyone who tasted it. Not poison, but it did work on vampires, or so Rhys was told. "And I imagine this explains your extraordinary luck luring women to your fold. By the rod of Min, Kilpatrick, you *do* have a ruthless streak, after all. Who would have thought?"

"I only use the herb on my enemies," Rhys retorted. He'd learned of the plant from a Sufi healer during his army days, and it had come in very handy on several occasions since then. But

...aid," Rhys said, refilling ... shaker. He wished ... erb sooner. Would the bas-... ve? "But my answer is the same as ... for the past hundred twenty-five years. No, thank you."

"Such a shame. I like you, Kilpatrick. But eventually you must die for your misguided loyalty."

"But not today!" a threatening voice growled from the front door as it was flung open. The house vibrated with the beginnings of a temblor.

Shahin.

Rhys turned to see his good friend storm in, black cloak swirling behind him like wings. "I'd come to warn you," Sheikh Shahin Aswadi said, halting under the onion-domed archway leading to the salon. "But I see I am too late."

The air crackled with the tension of gathering lightning. Shahin and Haru-Re glared at each other with bitter hatred. If Rhys didn't intervene there could well be a battle right here and now. Not that he didn't share Shahin's abhorrence of their foe. But he wasn't sure they could win against the more powerful demigod, even with two of them using all the magic they knew, as well as his friend's ability to call earthquakes.

"Shahin!" he greeted Seth's captain of the guard, going to him quickly. "*Ahlan, ahlan.* Come in and join us in a drink."

"Are you insa—"

"Rhys?"

The soft, hesitant female query brought the ex—change to an abrupt halt.

They all spun toward the sound.

Like a vision, Gillian stood in the mouth of the hallway leading to the master bedroom, barefoot and looking erotically disheveled. One delicate strap of her dress slid down a pale shoulder, exposing the curve of her milky breast.

His breath caught. *By the goddess Isis, she was beautiful.* He'd never seen anything so delicious in all his life.

A wave of power rolled through the room. *Immortal power.*

Or was it simply the power of stark male arousal…?

Just what was not needed in this already volatile male pissing contest.

If it had been Seth instead of Haru-Re standing in his salon, Rhys might despair of caution prevailing in the presence of such tempting feminine beauty. But as it was, he would die before he saw his enemy take her.

"Darling, come in." He opened his arms, compelling her to come to him, his own stiff cock reminding him not so subtly of all he had to lose should this go badly. As their bodies touched, he wove a spell of protection around her.

"I'm sorry," she said. "I must have…" She pushed her still-mussed hair from her sleepy eyes. "Oh! You have guests."

A streak of red stole across her cheeks as he brushed a kiss to her lips and folded her body

close to his, letting the other men know she belonged to him.

"Did you have a good nap, my dear?"

"Yes, I…" Her words faded in embarrassment.

So she remembered….

He smiled down at her. "Good. Wouldn't
want you fainting again." He leveled a look
at the high priest of the Lord of Sunrise and
said with a hint of irony, "Too much sun this
morning."

Haru-Re's arrogant gaze narrowed.

For a long moment Shahin stared at him and
Gillian in surprise. Rhys could almost hear the
gears turning behind his friend's hawk eyes.
Unfortunately, everything he must have been
thinking was true.

Haru-Re observed all this with cool calcu-
lation, then walked over to Gillian, grasped
her hand and bent over it in a courtly kiss.
"I'm Harold Ray, a…business acquaintance of
Rhys's. Call me Ray. Delighted to meet you,
Miss…?"

"Haliday," Rhys supplied curtly, deliberately leaving out her first name. She slanted a

questioning glance his way and he gave his head a grim shake. *Not a man you want to know.* "And this is my good friend Sheikh Shahin Aswadi."

Mumbling a nervous greeting to both men, she pulled her hand from Haru-Re's grip and straightened. "Obviously, I'm interrupting some kind of meeting between you gentlemen. I should be leaving anyway. My sisters—"

"The path is tricky. You'd never find your way," Rhys cut her off. "Why don't you call your sisters? Use the phone in my study."

"No, really, I—"

He sent a wave of influence over her. "Tell them you are staying with me tonight. You'll be back tomorrow."

"I…" Her face visibly relaxed. "All right."

"You like horses, don't you? Take a tour of my stables when you've finished on the phone. I'll meet you there when I'm done."

"Okay." He felt a spurt of pride and possessiveness when she tipped up her face to give him a shy kiss before she left. "Don't be long," she murmured.

"I won't be," he assured her. All three men

watched as she silently padded out of the room toward his study.

"You've bespelled her," Haru-Re said with amusement.

"What of it?" Rhys challenged. "She's mine to do with as I please."

The demigod tilted his head. "I was under the impression you didn't approve of the unwilling sexual coercion of mortals. Obviously, I've been gravely misinformed."

Rhys didn't comment. Let the man believe what he would. Shahin frowned.

"She looked familiar," Ray declared. "I am certain I've met your Miss Haliday before."

"I doubt that," Rhys refuted. "But her parents spent a lot of time in Egypt," he conceded carefully. "Perhaps you met them before they died."

The photo of Gillian's mother sifted through his mind. The man sitting next to Isobelle Haliday in his own courtyard had been one of Haru-Re's lieutenants, trying to win Rhys's friendship in order to infiltrate Khepesh. Had Haru-Re been hovering about that night, as well? Unfortunately, Rhys couldn't find and interrogate the lieutenant because when his deception was discovered the next day, Shahin had demonstrated his prowess at beheading a man with a single stroke of his scimitar. One of the surest ways to kill an immortal.

"Hmm." Ray sipped his martini. "It'll come to me."

"I'm sure it will," Rhys said, growing even more impatient. "Meanwhile, as you can see, I am otherwise occupied. So unless you have something pressing you wish to discuss…?"

To add bite to Rhys's words, Shahin spread his feet wide, planted his fists on his hips and fingered the silver hilt of his wickedly curved sword. The crystal glasses in the drinks cabinet began to tremble, making an incongruously cheerful tinkling sound.

Ray chuckled. "Control your quaking, Sheikh Shahin. Your eagerness to spill divine blood is showing. Don't you know the punishment for that in the afterlife?"

"There is a great difference between divine and immortal," Shahin growled, the tinkling growing louder. "I'm sure I would be amply rewarded for your head."

"Your black heart on the scales of Thot will be far heavier than my lowly head. I fear you will be the loser when the day of reckoning comes."

"Come, you two, I am in no mood to talk theology," Rhys interjected, attempting to move Haru-Re toward the front door. "I have a beautiful woman awaiting her mount in the stables. So if you've nothing more on your mind than to prove superior powers through irritation, I'll cede the win."

"As a matter of fact, I do," Ray said, standing his ground like an immovable obelisk. "You'll want to hear me out."

Rhys shared a brief look with Shahin. The glasses quieted. "All right. We're listening."

"I've come with an offer," Haru-Re said. "For Seth-Aziz."

Shahin barely masked a snort. "What could you possibly have to offer our master?"

Rhys raised a hand to silence him. Shahin was a fierce, awesome warrior, the best in the land, but his temper was too short for his own good sometimes. "What are you offering?"

"A truce. For five hundred years."

Shock stuttered through Rhys's veins, only to falter and fade to distrust. "In exchange for what?" *As if he didn't know.*

"The priestess Nephtys."

Shahin straightened like a shot, reaching for his scimitar. A shock wave rent through the room. "Never!"

Rhys put a restraining hand on his friend's shoulder, much like trying to restrain the wind. "Haru-Re, you must know Seth will never give you his sister."

"Not exclusively. I propose we share her, and her powers. It's hardly a secret I have no priestess left with the magic to grant immortality. I'm appealing to my rival's honor. For my people's sake. We need her help."

"Why would we grant you the means to survive," Shahin spat out, his voice gaining volume with each word, "when our sole purpose in life is to eradicate the infidel *shemsu* of Re-Horakhti from all Egypt?"

Haru-Re went rigid and fury swept over his features.

"Shahin!" Rhys snapped out a warning.

Too late. Bolts of brilliant light strobed from

Haru-Re's fingertips as they curled into fists. "I will not stand here and be insulted!"

"Perhaps you'd prefer to have your miserable existence ended instead." Shahin whipped out his curved sword and leaped forward as the whole room began to shake around them.

"'Tis not I who shall die but you!" Ray returned. He raised his hands and let loose a blinding barrage of light spears at Shahin just as the floor buckled under his feet, fouling his aim. Shahin's Bedouin robes swallowed him in a swirling tornado of black, and suddenly, in the blink of an eye, he was gone. A black hawk swooped out of nowhere and with a bloodcurdling cry circled Haru-Re, who lifted his hands and—

Behind them a woman screamed.

Chapter 8

I am he who cometh forth as one who
breaketh through the door;
and everlasting is the Nighttime which his
will hath created.

—*The Papyrus of Ani*

Gillian could not believe the things her mind
was telling her she'd just witnessed.

A man—Rhys's friend—had turned into
a hawk! Right here, before her very eyes. His
human body had simply vanished, the hawk
emerging from the place where he had been

an instant before. Like something out of one of Gemma's fantastic legends…

Impossible!

And that other man, the sinister-looking Harold Ray, the light that surrounded him was blinding. And he was *shooting fire from his fingers*.

None of this was possible!

Ray whipped around and spotted her. Instantly, the fire disappeared. But his face— She'd never seen anyone so angry. *He looked like he wanted to kill her.* The hawk swooped in a tight circle around the room with an other-worldly cry, then arrowed out through the open courtyard doors, momentarily distracting him.

She pressed her hands over her mouth to keep from screaming again.

She must be going crazy. Or had hit her head on the stone floor of the tomb when she'd fainted. Or gotten sunstroke, as Rhys suggested. She'd been acting so strange all afternoon, so unlike herself…. And now this…utter insanity! It must be magic tricks. Illusions, that was all.

She didn't know what was happening here, but one thing she did know.

She had to get out of this place.

She turned to flee, heading for the front door.

"Gillian!" In less than a split second Rhys was in front of her. He caught her in his strong grip.

She fought him. "Let me go!" She kicked and clawed at her captor. "Let me *go!*"

"Give her to me," Harold Ray ordered, between teeth that seemed to be growing long and sharp. He reached for her. "I'll take care of the little spy."

"No!" she squeaked, fighting harder.

Rhys swept her away from the other man's grasp. "Leave her! And leave my house!"

"But she has seen—"

"I'll deal with it," Rhys snapped.

Gillian continued to struggle, but it was no use. Her captor had preternatural strength. She swallowed an hysterical sob. *God help her.*

Ray visibly calmed, settling his body as a bird might do after ruffling his feathers. "And my proposal?"

"I will convey it," Rhys said, still holding on to her mercilessly.

"See that you do," the other man said. "And

remind your master that to use the priestess against my people will take time. Time he doesn't have. Right now my forces are vastly superior to his. If Seth-Aziz turns me down, I will have no option but to use them. Soon."

Gillian shook uncontrollably. Master? Seth-Aziz? What the hell were they talking about? The cult of Set-Sutekh again? Or some kind of terrorism?

"One week, Englishman. I'll return for my answer in seven days," Ray said, his gaze gliding menacingly toward her. She cowered behind Rhys's back, reluctantly accepting his offered protection. "And to give you a little extra incentive to plead my case, if you don't bring me the answer I want, I'll make sure your pretty little plaything is my first hostage."

Gillian gasped at his cruel laugh.

He strode for the door. "Her life is in your hands, Kilpatrick. Don't disappoint me." He turned with a parting sneer over his shoulder. "Or her."

Gillian prayed she wouldn't faint again. It was actually the first time today she really *felt* like fainting. The other times, the light-

headedness had come over her out of the clear
blue. But this…

"You'd better sit down," Rhys broke through
her paralysis, and she realized Harold Ray had
gone, along with the mysterious black hawk.
The room was quiet as a tomb.

Oh, God. Bad choice of words.

Why, oh, why had she ventured into that stupid tomb in the first place? Next time she would
definitely listen to Mehmet. If she got a next
time…

Rhys led her to a silk-covered divan, pushing
aside a pile of tapestry cushions, and pulled her
to sit down next to him.

She tried to scramble away, to the other end
of the settee, but he held on. "There's nothing to
be afraid of. He won't be back," Rhys said, but
she was hardly reassured by the somber look on
his face.

She let out a strangled laugh, wrapping her
free arm around her middle. "Who…*what* are
you people?"

"We'll get to that." He exhaled a long breath.
"But you must understand, I can't let you go
now."

"What?" Her heart quailed, her pulse speeding out of control. They *were* terrorists! Or some kind of dangerous cult of magicians. She shook her head desperately. "I won't tell anyone about your tricks. I swear I won't. Not a soul. Who'd believe me, anyway?"

He regarded her, almost sadly. "I can't take that chance. For your own safety, as much as mine."

"You can't keep me here!" Frightened tears pressed at her eyes. "My sisters will—"

"Won't come for you. You phoned them earlier to say you are staying with me."

She suddenly remembered doing that. Though heaven knew why. She'd never had any intention of— "My God, you *drugged* me. Or hypnotized me!" That would explain the fainting, the wanton behavior and the weird hallucinations.

He took her trembling hands. "Not hypnosis. I bespelled you. And your sisters. Which is why they'll never come looking for you. Ever."

Her tears threatened to spill over. Tears of confusion.

She couldn't believe what he was saying. "Be*spelled*? Are you kidding? They *will* come for me!" she insisted. Nothing on earth would stop them from searching for her. Just as nothing had stopped the three of them from searching for their vanished parents.

"Then your sisters will be captured, as well," he returned.

Captured? Despair swept through her. She was right! "No!"

He smiled gently. "It's not such a terrible fate. In fact, I'd hoped…darling, I'd truly hoped you'd come willingly with me."

"Willingly?" She stared at him incredulously, the errant thought careening through her mind that just an hour ago she might actually have considered— "To be a terrorist? Or a kidnapper, or…" *Or worse.*

His mouth parted, his expression puzzled, then it cleared. "Ah. So that is what you think. No, Gillian. I assure you, I'm not a criminal or a terrorist. I detest violence. I much prefer…a friendlier persuasion."

He gazed at her with those thick-lashed bedroom eyes and she nearly forgot why she was so upset. She *did* forget when he leaned forward and touched his lips to hers. It was like his touch robbed her of every self-protective instinct she had. All she felt was want. She closed her eyes and a million erotic sensations pulsed through her body, urging her to open to him, to surrender to him, to—

"No!" She jumped up from the divan, surprising the hell out of them both. "I'll not be bespelled, as you call it, by your kisses. Not again!"

He leaned back on the sofa and a grin spread over his far too handsome face. "Is that how you think I ensnared your will? With my kiss?"

Heat crept through her. Embarrassment, mixed with a hot lick of intense arousal. And a sizzle of apprehension. "Wasn't it?"

"No. But it's nice to know you are so susceptible to my charms." He patted the cushion next to him, beckoning with those wicked eyes, and despite everything, she had to fight the overwhelming desire to go to him. To let him win all over again.

Jesus. Maybe the man *did* have powers. Or was really good at hypnosis.

She took a cleansing breath. "I will *not* be your sex toy, Rhys. And there are laws against kidnapping, even in Egypt. You can't keep me here against my will."

The grin vanished and a muscle ticked below his eye. "Nor would I want that. When I take a woman to my bed it's because she wants me as much as I want her."

"So, earlier, you didn't…influence me in any way?"

He hesitated for the briefest second. "I may have enhanced your pleasure. But not your desire. That was all yours."

Not exactly news.

He rose in a lithe movement. "You may not believe this, but I was trying desperately *not* to touch you."

She gazed uncertainly at the tall, powerful man who stood before her. And suddenly realized she had no memory of anything after experiencing that amazing climax he'd given her. That's when she'd fainted. *Again*. Had he not completed the act?

"Why not?" she asked, and for some reason was afraid of the answer.

He gazed down at her for a moment, then turned abruptly and paced away. "Because first

you must know the truth about me. About...
everything."

The way he said it, solemnly, almost grimly,
made her pulse take off at a run. She had a hor-
rible feeling that she did not *want* to know the
truth about him. Or anything. That what he was
about to say would alter her life forever, would
change her completely, irrevocably, in some un-
imagined way.

But the empty void between her legs still
throbbed from his touch, still ached for him to
fill it, and her, with everything her life and her
heart were missing. How could she want a man
who was bad? She couldn't. Could she?

She had to know.

"Who are you?" she tremulously asked. "And
why have you kidnapped me?"

He turned to face her. Captured her eyes with
his. A strange, powerful energy pulsed through
the air, raising the hairs on her arms, electrify-
ing her body with apprehension.

"I am a follower of Set-Sutekh," he said,
his deep voice echoing through the room, "I
am master steward to Seth-Aziz, high priest to

the god. And you, Gillian Haliday, have been chosen to become our next initiate."

"Me?" Terror sizzled over her skin like goose bumps. *Ohgod-ohgod-ohgod.* The cult, this *per netjer* he talked about, *did* still exist. And she was about to disappear forever. "Why me?"

He leveled his gaze upon her. "Because, my darling, as I said, you know too much. You found the secret way into the tomb. You witnessed Shahin shift. And you've attracted the attention of our enemy, putting yourself in mortal danger." His voice went deeper still. "But most of all, because we need you. For our most sacred ceremony."

"What ceremony?" she asked, shaking uncontrollably at the otherworldly glitter reflected in his eyes.

"Our god Set-Sutekh requires an annual sacrifice. This year, your body shall provide that sacrifice."

"My *body?*" she squeaked. Sweet mercy. He was deadly serious.

"More specifically, your blood."

A noise of pure horror escaped her. This was going too far. "You can't kill me!" she cried, springing to her feet. Time to go. Away from him. From this complete insanity. But there was no getting past him. He was immovable. Like the pyramids.

"Kill you?" he said calmly, grasping her hands. "No, Gillian. In fact, we plan to do quite the opposite."

She could barely form the words for dread. "What do you mean?"

"When you give yourself over to the god," he said softly, "the sacrifice you make is not your life. It is your *death*."

She stared at him, shaking, uncomprehending. "I don't understand."

He slid his hands gently up to her shoulders. Gazed deep into her eyes. "Join us willingly, Gillian. Offer your service to the god and become like me," he urged.

"Like you how?" she asked. "What in God's name *are* you, Rhys?"

He leaned in, put his lips to her ear, and whispered, *"I am immortal."*

Chapter 9

I let you hear my voice cry out
for my myrrh-anointed beauty,
and you were with me there
when I prepared my trap.

—*The Song of the Harper*

Gillian's body shuddered, then she stood absolutely, utterly still for a long, long time.

Rhys probably shouldn't have been surprised that when she finally moved, it was to close her eyes, take a deep, trembling breath, and say, "*So* not funny, Rhys. But I have to admit, you really had me going there." Her eyes opened with a scowl. "*Immortal?* Jesus, give me a freaking break. You are one sick puppy, and I *am* leaving now," she said evenly. "Do. Not. Try to stop me."

Osiris preserve him.

"It's true, Gillian. All of it. And there's more."

She marched toward the door, waving a hand over her shoulder. "Seriously? I don't want to hear it."

He folded his own hands behind his back to keep from grabbing her. "Perhaps you've forgotten what you just saw happen here in this very room. Haru-Re shooting spears of light? How about when Shahin transformed himself into a hawk? Just how would you explain all of that?"

"Obviously some kind of trickery. Illusions and stories designed to persuade impressionable young women into your bed and your cult. You just chose the wrong victim."

Talk about denial. "You are not a victim, Gillian. And I didn't need any trickery to persuade you into my bed," he reminded her. "You came all on your own."

She blushed. "A mistake which won't be repeated."

"Very well. But what about the photo of your mother? Would you so readily give up a chance to find out what happened to her? Join us, and Nephtys will help you. I give you my word."

She kept walking. "I'm just not that gullible, Rhys. There are no such things as immortals, shape-shifters or fortune-tellers. You're welcome to enjoy your bizarre little cult, but I want no part of it."

Rhys cringed, glad the immortals of Khepesh were not here to hear the unflattering epithets. He feared Gillian would pay dearly for such insults.

He tried a different tack. "Gillian, you're not really planning to hike through the desert all the way to Naqada by yourself, and dressed like that, are you?"

That stopped her. She looked down at the gorgeous but insubstantial, flowing dress he'd given her, and her bare feet.

She turned, her mouth pressed in a thin line. "Where are my own clothes?"

"As I recall, littering the floor of my study."

Her flush deepened. He couldn't help but feel a burst of smugness. At his expression, her chin went up and she started marching toward the hall, presumably to go and change. This time he didn't stop himself. He closed the distance between them in two strides.

"Stop!" he ordered when she struggled against his hold. "Shh." He waited until her resistance ceased, then murmured, "*You* took off your clothes for me, Gillian. *You* let me taste your body. You trusted me enough to do that, and much more."

"That was…before," she said. "I didn't know."

"Didn't know what?" He forced her chin up, so she had no choice but to look at him. "Didn't know *what,* Gillian?"

Dismay clouded her green eyes. And something more… Attraction.

He dipped under her hem and slowly ran his hand up her thigh and over her bare hip, caressed the smooth curve of her bottom. *She'd stayed naked for him under the dress.*

"I could take you right now. You'd let me. We both know it."

She didn't deny his claim. How could she?

With an unhappy groan, she wrapped her fingers around his upper arms and tried to push him away. To hide her body's reaction to his words, to his touch. *Too late.* He felt the alabaster hardness of her nipples, the sultry heat of her skin. And smelled the perfume of her desire.

"Trust me," he whispered. "Trust me to bring you to a wondrous palace where Set-Sutekh's immortals live in sensual splendor forever. Come to Khepesh with me. See it for yourself. Then decide if you will join us or not."

Her voice hitched. "These things are impossible, Rhys. What you say is impossible."

He searched her disbelieving eyes. "Is it? Let me prove it to you. All of it. You have nothing to lose, and eternity to gain."

"And what of this blood sacrifice you talked about?" she asked. "It's crazy, and I don't want any part of it."

At the mention of the ceremony, he tamped down a renewed surge of jealousy. It was the last thing he wanted, too. The thought of Seth drinking her blood, touching her body was unbearable. But they would both get through it.

"It's just a small amount of blood. Nothing dangerous. And do you remember the pleasure I gave you earlier?"

She swallowed. Averted her gaze and nodded.

"The pleasure of the ritual is a thousand times greater." Which was true. Unfortunately, it wouldn't be Rhys bestowing it. He wanted to howl with frustration, but he knew his duty. First and foremost it was to Seth-Aziz, his friend, his leader.

"Come with me," he murmured seductively. He had to get her to Khepesh. Afterward he would find a way to change Seth's mind.

She nibbled her lip. Tempted. But skeptical. "This is totally insane. None of what you say is physically possible."

"But what if it is?" he murmured, and waited. "What if I am truly offering you a chance for immortality? Would you pass it up so easily?"

He could see she was wavering. From sheer curiosity, if nothing else. "If…if I consent to trust you," she asked, "to let you show me these things you speak of, if I still want to leave, will you then let me go?"

"You won't want to," he assured her, certain

of the lure of the powers she would be granted. As well as the temptation of himself… That last was possibly a cruel deception, but at this point there was no way around it. The solace was that he would be as upset as she if they were ultimately denied each other.

But he had already told her the truth of the matter. She belonged to Khepesh now, willing or no. After discovering the tomb entrance, and especially after Haru-Re's threat and witnessing Shahin's shift to hawk, Seth would never let her go. Not alive. Nothing in Rhys's power could change that.

"I promise to help you discover what became of your mother," he added. Though, all indications were that she would not like what she was bound to learn. Not if Haru-Re was involved.

"But no blood, Rhys. I mean it."

"Not if I have any say in the matter," he vowed, and meant it, though ultimately he had little say in that, either.

"Okay," she finally acceded, though reluctance still tugged at her. "I'll come with you. But just for a look."

He smiled and kissed her, wrapping his conscience in the silken heat of her response.

He pulled her close, pressing into her belly with the fierce erection that had again grown thick and long from want of her. *A stallion's erection.* She gave a soft exhale at its bold prodding at her soft flesh.

He groaned low. "Feel how I deny myself to win you over."

After a second, the tension slowly left her body and she relaxed against him, easing out a sigh. "How can I be so terrified of you, Rhys Kilpatrick, and so damned attracted to you at the same time?"

He smiled into her hair, breathing in the scent of her. "Maybe you like your lovers dark and dangerous."

"I never have before," she confessed, making him wonder how many men she'd had. Not many, he'd wager.

"Which might explain the absence of a man in your life."

He felt her wince. "For the moment."

"That is about to change," he promised, pressing a kiss to her temple.

He just prayed he would be the one to change it.

"But first," he said, pulling away before he gave in and did what his body was urging him to do, but which he would surely live to regret, "are you ready?"

"For what?"

"For me to blow your notion of reality all to hell."

"Sister, what troubles you?"

Nephtys tore her gaze from the amethyst amulet she held in her fingers and forced a smile to her lips. "No troubles, *hadu*," she said, turning away from the enchanted glass through which she had been gazing at the sun and sky in the desert above the underground palace. "Quite the opposite. I have had a vision."

A frown sketched her brother's forehead when he saw what she held. Seth knew it had been a gift from Haru-Re. A scarab made of the finest purple amethyst with his cartouche carved on its belly, given to her the morning after he'd taken her virginity. A meager payment, but more than any of his other slaves had ever received. She'd worn it faithfully until his callous betrayal. Now she only brought it out when trouble brewed. Seth hated the sight of it.

Thankfully, instead of scolding her, he asked, "Oh? Anything interesting in your vision?"

She slipped the amulet into the pocket of her caftan and reached for his hands. This time her smile was genuine. "Wonderful news. I have seen her. Your future consort."

His eyes lit. "Tell me what you saw."

"Indications are she is wise, and will become a favorite of the people. She's also quite beautiful. A blonde, you'll be happy to hear," she added, knowing his taste in women ran to pale and elegant.

Seth's attention sharpened. "A blonde, you say. Would you know this woman again?"

"Of course. Why? Do you know of a possibility?"

"Lord Kilpatrick has marked a new initiate. He will arrive with her soon. It's why I came to fetch you. We should meet them at the Western Gate."

She nodded. "Give me a moment to prepare. I'll join you there."

He started to turn away, then stopped and looked back at her, letting his gaze slip down to the pocket of her caftan. "Did you see him, too?" he asked. "In this vision?"

She swallowed. And shook her head. "No," she said. Well, she hadn't. And there was no use worrying Seth with conjecture. "Not for a long time now." She pulled a smile from somewhere.

His eyes searched hers for a long moment, no doubt sensing she was keeping some inner torment from him. Too perceptive, as always. "Why do you continue to torture yourself, my little sister? It pains me to see you suffer over a man who would destroy you and all you love without a thought."

She struggled against the emotion, holding it back from finding cracks in her resolve. "I know," she said. "You are my brother, my dearest and only family, and I am so grateful for all you have given me. All you have done for me. I hate him for betraying me. But I hate him more for wanting to take me from you and Khepesh."

"I'll never let him. You know that."

"I swear I would die before I served him against you."

Her adopted brother smiled kindly at her and kissed her cheek. "I've never doubted it, *habibi*." He sighed. "It should be you at my side as consort," he said. "Not some strange woman I have yet to meet."

She wrinkled her nose. "Marrying one's sister may have been the way of the pharaohs, but I've seen you in too many preposterously compromising positions even to entertain the notion of sharing your bed."

He pretended to be affronted, but his grin gave him away. "I should smite you for your impertinence, woman." He leaned over her. "At the very least a good spanking."

She poked his chest. "*That's* exactly what I'm talking about. I'm not into kinky sex."

He snorted.

Her mouth dropped open, scandalized at the implication of that rude noise. *"You!"*

"I could shift myself to look like my enemy while we couple," he suggested cheekily.

He laughed as she attacked him, fending off her fists and slaps until they both dissolved into giggles in each other's arms. The thought of Seth shifting into the other man's likeness was outrageous. *He* would rather die.

She cleared her throat. "I appreciate the consideration, brother, but I'd rather sleep with a rabid jackal than give myself to Haru-Re again, real or not." She extracted herself from their tangle of arms and smoothed her gown, attempting to regain her sisterly dignity. "And as for being your consort, I'd rather marry a flatulent water buffalo. No offense," she added with a final lopsided grin.

After a bark of laughter at her declaration, he assured her affectionately, "None taken."

As usual, he'd known exactly how to tease her from her blue mood. To his flock, Seth-Aziz was ever the regal, somber, autocratic high priest who'd steadfastly led them through five millennia of triumphs and disasters. But to Nephtys, he would always be the dear, fun-loving practical joker she'd grown up with.

"Come," he invited her. "Let us go and meet my new bride and welcome her into our family."

She smiled. "Try and keep me away."

She took his arm and followed him out of the temple and down the long hall toward the Great Western Gate. To her consternation, with every step she took, the heavy amethyst amulet in her pocket bounced against her thigh. An unwelcome reminder of the ugly conflicts that lay ahead on the horizon.

Perhaps this new initiate, the woman destined to be Seth's consort and mistress of Khepesh, would help them win the coming battle. For against Haru-Re, Nephtys herself was bound to lose every time.

The sun was a fiery ball of orange that hung just above the *gebel* as Gillian followed Rhys out to the stables. She tried desperately not to think about what might happen now. She didn't believe a word he'd said. Except about his attraction to her, which was obviously genuine. As was hers for him. This cult—this *per netjer*—thing scared her. And the talk of blood sacrifices. But it was the part about her mother that kept her from walking away. She was certain he knew more about that photo than he was telling. Had her mother gotten involved in the *per netjer* Rhys spoke of? If so, why wouldn't Rhys just tell her? Why the elaborate setup? She owed it to herself and her sisters to find out the truth.

The heat of the day was waning, cooled by the deep shade of the vertical sandstone cliffs surrounding Rhys's estate on three sides. It was the first time she'd seen it from the outside. The place was incredibly beautiful.

Done in traditional Moorish architecture, the house and outbuildings were works of art. Delicate arches and soaring columns were decorated with tasteful mosaic tile work and punctuated by bubbling fountains and giant ceramic pots spilling lush greenery and exotic-smelling flowers.

Even the stables looked as though they should house royalty, rather than mere horses. Gillian wondered what could possibly be found inside that Rhys was so determined she should see. To be honest, at the moment she was far more interested in studying the man himself. Crazy or not, he was undeniably a stud.

Before leaving the house he'd donned his outer cloak, which swirled about him like a black whirlwind as he walked. Along with his black tunic, breeches and knee-high leather boots, he also wore a long black keffiyeh head-dress, shot through here and there with silver threads, held in place on his head by a thick, multistranded silver *agal*. He looked incredible. Like some impossibly sexy Bedouin sheikh.

In nothing but the gossamer turquoise dress that kept falling off her shoulders and a pair of delicate silver sandals he'd given her, she feared she fit the part all too well of a helpless, captive slave girl destined for his harem.

Which really should have worried her more than it did. But somehow she had managed to lock away her fears and give him the trust he'd asked of her. For now, at any rate. If he meant to harm her, surely he'd have done so by now. He'd had ample opportunity. But instead, he'd given her pleasures such as she'd never experienced before in her life. And promised far more.

To her surprise, he led her straight through the cool, dark interior of the stables, which smelled of sweet hay and tangy alfalfa, past several stable hands who bowed and lowered their eyes respectfully as she passed, and out into a carefully tended grassy meadow.

A servant appeared at the bàrn door holding a thin rope. Rhys waved him off. The servant bowed and disappeared again.

Rhys took her to the center of the pasture and let go of her hand, then backed away. His amber eyes studied her, his expression giving away none of his thoughts.

"With the sun behind you, I can see right through your dress," he remarked. "Your body is breathtaking. You look like a golden-haired temple maiden from the days of the pharaohs."

Heat suffused her cheeks, but in pleasure. It should bother her that he was practically drinking in her nakedness, but it didn't. She had abandoned her modesty hours ago with this man. She could still feel his tongue between her legs.

"And you look like a romantic sheikh straight out of an old black-and-white movie," she returned warmly.

His lips curved. "I'm much taller than Rudy Valentino."

"And way sexier," she murmured.

She'd also given up pretending she didn't want him. Dangerous con man, cult fanatic or plain nut-case, Rhys Kilpatrick was walking, talking, knee-melting sex, and she wanted more of him.

His nostrils flared. "Darling, you are making it very difficult for me to resist ravishing you on the spot."

She tilted her head and arched her brows in invitation.

He wagged his finger at her. "You are a very naughty girl." Not that he seemed in the least bit upset about that. "But you will not distract me from my purpose. Not yet."

She gave a moue. Maybe if she let the dress slide all the way off...

"Are you ready for a ride?" he asked.

She smiled. *More like it.* She took a step toward him. "Oh, yes."

"Good." He grasped her by the hips. "Whatever happens, hold on tight."

Okaaay... She melted into him with a flutter of illicit excitement, prepared to wrap her legs around his waist and be ravished. Or ravish him if he didn't hurry up. "I will."

She felt herself being lifted, but to her surprise, instead of lifting her dress and impaling her on his mouth-wateringly huge erection, he swung her around to his back and joined her hands at the base of his throat, then slipped his own hands around her thighs.

"Hang on!" he called and twirled once like a dervish, his robes wrapping about them both like a whirling black cocoon, and chanting some strange—

What the—

All at once his body began to grow bigger, and harder, and bigger still, and then bucked and bent over double so she was sitting astride his back, but…high up in the air.

She cried out and grabbed fistfuls of his hair to keep from toppling off. It was long and coarse in her fingers, not his hair at all, but…a horse's mane! And suddenly she realized she was sitting astride not a man but a huge, coal-black stallion.

Oh, sweet Jesus. Just as Shahin had changed into a hawk, Rhys's body had shifted into that of a horse.

It raised its head and trumpeted a deafening

equine call, lifting up onto its hind legs, forelegs pumping in the air. She bent low over its neck and hung on for dear life, shaking with shock and terror.

Her mind rebelled.

It wasn't possible.

It wasn't *possible*.

It wasn't possible!

But the evidence between her knees was impossible to ignore, impossible to deny.

Rhys had shifted himself from man to beast!

And that was when it hit her.

My God! Al Fahl. The black stallion up on the *gebel!*

The one who'd watched her so intently even then, sending chills of awareness through her body.

Al Fahl. The ghost stallion was *Rhys!*

Chapter 10

Oh, might I welcome you
as the king's own steed is welcome,
thoroughbred, best in the stables!
How well the heart of a girl can feel it
(charge on and on, my lovely stallion!)
when her love's not far away.
  —*Love song,* Papyrus Chester Beatty I

Al Fahl rode the burning wind of the Western Desert, flying with his prize clinging to his back, up, up the soaring sandstone *gebel* to the desolate plateau above, galloping over hot sands into the flaming orb of the setting sun, taking the woman to meet her destiny.

The woman he wanted for himself.

At the hidden entrance to Khepesh, he came to a clattering halt and reared up, letting out a whinnying cry of triumph as he turned on his hind legs and brought forth the transformation unto his flesh, so he was once more a man.

Rhys reached around and caught Gillian before she slid from his back to the shadowing ground.

"My God, my *God!*" she sobbed over and over as he lifted her in his arms to carry her. She blinked up at him in abject horror, trying desperately to push him away. "What *are* you? What in God's name *are you?*"

"I told you. I am one of Set-Sutekh's immortals," he said, sending a calming spell over her. "As such, I have the ability to shape-shift. I chose a stallion as my *ka* body."

"Al Fahl," she said with an all too clear understanding of what that implied.

"Yes," he admitted. "A convenient mythology, but it's a bit embarrassing to have such an unsavory reputation out there." Now was probably not the time to tell her that much of it was true. At least it had been. "Feeling better yet?"

"No," she said, more forcefully than her limp state would signify. "Put me down. Please."

"I shouldn't trust your legs right now."

He strode to the entrance of the rock-hewn stairway that descended into the underground tomb-palace of Khepesh and waved his hand over it, uttering the opening incantation. When the chasm of stone opened, he plunged down into the darkness, taking two steps at a time.

Gillian twisted in his arms, panic radiating from every pore. "Where are you taking me? Let me *go*."

Obviously the calming spell wasn't working.

"Darling, we've talked about this. You know where we're going. There's nothing to worry about. I swear you won't be harmed. You promised to trust me, remember?"

"This was not part of the bargain! I thought… God, I don't know what I thought. But not this!"

"Believe me, I know it's a lot to take in. I went through it all myself." He halted on a wide step and lowered her to her feet, but kept her body pressed close to his, just in case she tried to bolt.

The tunnel was dark as night. As a denizen of the underworld he was used to it. He didn't have to see her face to know what she was feeling. He could smell the fear in her shallow breaths, feel the doubts in her trembling limbs and the need to escape in the clamminess of her hands as she clung to him in the blackness.

"You won't be sorry, Gillian. You can have life without end, gifted with powers you've never even dreamed of."

She let out a soft sob. "What if I don't want powers, or to live forever?"

"Don't be absurd. Everyone wants to live forever."

The tension of her grip increased. "That depends on what one is expected to do during all that time, doesn't it?"

Wise beyond her years, this one. It had taken him half a century to figure that out.

"It's simple. You must serve our god, Set-Sutekh, and our leader, the High Priest Seth-

Aziz. Apart from those few duties, your life can be your own."

"I'm not a pagan, Rhys. I only believe in one God."

"And yet you pour libations to the local spirits when you eat. I've seen you and your sisters perform this rite."

She choked out a strangled curse. "I didn't say I wasn't superstitious."

He kissed her temple. "I'm a Christian just like you, Gillian. But once you see the powers of these ancient gods, you won't be able to deny their existence, either. I believe we all merely serve different aspects of God's incredible creation. I don't see it as a contradiction."

"You've been living in Egypt too long," she said unhappily. "Everything here is a contradiction."

"So you agree to come and see for yourself?"

She was silent for a long moment. "I'm afraid, Rhys," she whispered.

"I understand. I was, too, the first time I entered Khepesh. But when I saw the wonders, heard what would be granted me, felt the power I could possess, I knew I'd found my home."

"I suppose…it wouldn't hurt to look."

"There is just one stipulation," he told her.

He felt her tense again. "The sacrifice?"

"Other than that." He ran his hand down her back. "You must come to us willingly."

"Before or after I've seen it?"

"Both."

"And if I'm not willing? If I don't want to stay?"

Oh, she would be staying, all right. *One way or another.*

He didn't really want to think about the alternative. Unwilling mortals who had seen or learned too much were turned to *shabti,* robbed of their will and made human servants, well-treated but unable to retain their former personality or a will of their own. It was a loathsome practice Rhys had been fighting for most of his tenure as master steward. But he knew the only other option for an unwilling initiate was to meet with some kind of fatal accident.

Neither was an acceptable fate for Gillian. He wanted her alive and vibrant and able to say no. There was little joy in a conquest who had no power to deny him.

As for the ceremony…Seth needed a blood sacrifice, but it didn't necessarily have to be Gillian. Nor did Seth have to take her body as part of the ritual. There were plenty of others in the palace who would jump at the chance to serve as sacrificial vessel. Rhys would just have to persuade him to choose someone else.

But either way, Gillian must be brought to Khepesh. And his job was to see it done.

In the darkness, he bent down and sought her lips with his. He brushed over them softly. "Never doubt it, you are already willing, my sweet," he murmured. "Now, let us go."

"Promise not to leave me?" she whispered, clinging to him.

"I'll be there for you, Gillian. Always. That much I swear."

And silently he prayed he'd be allowed to keep that promise.

Gillian took Rhys's hand and blindly followed him down, down into the blackest void she'd ever experienced…other than the tomb where she'd first encountered Rhys. Was this the same eerie tomb? He kept calling it a palace. But weren't palaces aboveground? This felt like entering the Underworld. The only thing keeping her from dissolving into unmitigated panic was the feel of his strong, unrelenting fingers clasping hers.

"Let your instincts guide you," he told her when she stumbled for the fourth time. "Your feet know where to step. Don't think about it, just close off your mind and let your senses show you the way."

"Easy for you to say," she muttered, and in her hand as he squeezed it, she felt his smile.

But she gave it a try, and amazingly, she stopped stumbling. They walked on and on, the air around them growing cool and sweetly spicy as they went deeper and deeper into the earth. Compared to the blazing heat above, it felt surprisingly good. With no other sensory input, she lost track of all direction, all sense of time and space.

After what could have been five minutes or twenty-five, suddenly out of the darkness in front of them loomed a huge double door blocking the tunnel. Glittering silver and flanked by tall, lotus-shaped, burning torches, it soared at least three stories above them, making her squint against the brightness after the stygian tunnel. When her eyes adjusted, she saw that both wings of the monumental door were decorated in intricate hieroglyphics. She recognized the cartouches of Set-Sutekh that graced the center of each, and to her shock, the same left Eye of Horus as on Mehmet's amulet. After that, she couldn't concentrate to decipher the rest of the inscription. She was too freaked out by the sight of it all. Hell, by the whole astonishing experience. She had a hard time believing any of what had happened to her today. She'd tried telling herself she was still knocked out, dreaming in that dratted tomb, and that Mehmet would arrive any moment to awaken her and take her back to her sisters. But she had the sinking feeling that wasn't going to happen.

Her anxiety skyrocketed when the portal resonated with a long, deep clang, and slowly started to open.

"Welcome to Khepesh," Rhys said, his eyes

gleaming an unnatural red in the flames of the torches.

She shivered. *Oh, God, what had she done?* Was he a devil? Was this Hell? Like Persephone, was she really about to descend into the realm of the Underworld?

She tried to extract her hand from his, to run away through the blackness, back up to the familiar light of the desert surface.

But he wouldn't let his grip on her slacken. "Steady on," he admonished quietly.

What had she been thinking? "I've changed my mind," she blurted out, panic sweeping over her with a vengeance. Okay, she didn't believe in Hades…or anything else she'd seen today, even though to deny it would be admitting she'd lost her mind for real…but this was way too creepy.

"Too late," he said.

She spun in the direction of his gaze. Standing in the bright gape of the monumental entry gate were a half hundred people, all dressed in gorgeous attire and staring at her with varying degrees of curiosity. A tall, regal man stood in their midst, a beautiful redheaded woman next to him. From his aura of steely authority and his splendid robes, Gillian guessed he was the man in charge. The modern-day Seth-Aziz? Rather than curious, his expression was more like…gratified. Was the woman next to him the seer Rhys had spoken of?

"My lord," Rhys said with a formal bow, confirming one of her suspicions. "I am returned from above with the captive, as promised." He motioned to her and intoned, "On your knees, woman, and bow before your lord and master, Seth-Aziz, Immortal Guardian of Darkness, high priest to the Lord of the Night Sky!"

Gillian's eyes widened, spooling back Rhys's rhetoric. There was that word again. *Captive.* Had he lied to her after all?

Before she knew what was happening, she found herself kneeling just outside the gate, under intense scrutiny by the gathering of onlookers. But especially by Seth-Aziz and his flame-haired companion. A rash of goose bumps rose along Gillian's arms. Immortal shape-shifter or crazy cult leader? She wasn't sure which would be worse….

She squirmed uncomfortably under their gaze, crossing her arms over her body, embarrassed by the near-transparency of the dress Rhys had given her. Why had she not remembered to change clothes before coming?

"It is she!" the red-haired woman cried, clearly pleased. "The woman from my vision!"

A low murmur rippled through the crowd. Seth-Aziz's eyes returned to Gillian, taking her in again from head to knee. A smile slowly spread across his quite handsome face. "Excellent! You have done well, Lord Kilpatrick. She will make a succulent sacrifice and a worthy consort. What is her name?"

Hold on. *Consort?* No, no. *Hell,* no.

"Gillian Haliday, my lord," Rhys answered respectfully.

"And she comes willingly to us?"

She opened her mouth to set the record straight and tell him no damn way would she have any part of this newest insanity, but Rhys shot her a fierce warning glance. "Yes. She is willing."

"And the family, the sisters you spoke of?"

"Dealt with."

Alarm zinged through her. He'd mentioned bespelling, but could he mean something more sinister? Again, Rhys warned her off with a penetrating look. She wanted to cry out in protest! To demand to know what he'd really done to them. But the palpable power emanating from the leader Seth-Aziz brushed over her skin in waves, raising the fine hairs and convincing her she should trust Rhys's counsel, and heed it. She had to be careful.

It went against everything in her to remain silent, but she did. For now. She would grill him later.

Was she being stupid by trusting a virtual stranger? Making the biggest mistake of her life? Getting herself into something for which there was no way out? It seemed more and more likely. One look at the faces around her and she knew she was in too deep to back out now.

Thoughts of her mother seared through her mind. Had she also been confronted by a fatal choice years ago? Not by the lure of the *per netjer* or a dark lover—Mama had loved Daddy to distraction, had never even looked at another man and hadn't believed in organized religion, legit or not. But maybe the enticement had been something closer to home, like the promise of a fabulous archaeological find. A lost pharaoh's tomb...*or a demigod's.*

Or perhaps eternal life...? Gillian could see that being a temptation to one who loved life with such a passion. Had the whisper of immortality been enough for Mama to desert her precious family? The man in the photo—had he been her mother's harbinger of everlasting life? Had he perhaps threatened her children, her husband, if she refused to join the cult?

Impossible choices.

All this rushed through Gillian's mind as the high priest stepped forward through the parted crowd. Rhys left her kneeling before the gigantic doors and went to stand at his leader's side, opposite the seer-priestess.

"If you would join us, Gillian Haliday, and become one of Set-Sutekh's immortals," Seth-Aziz bid her in a booming command. "Rise and walk through the portal and meet your destiny!"

By now many more people had gathered around the entrance to the palace. They all watched her expectantly. Rhys nodded almost imperceptibly. It was clear what he wanted her to do.

Lord help her.

Could she really go through with this?

Wasn't it all too insane? Too ridiculously dangerous?

And yet, at this point what choice did she have? Cult crazies or the vastly unlikely remnants of an ancient race of immortals, these people were not going to just let her walk away. That was obvious by the scatter of muscular armed guards that had quietly rimmed the periphery of the crowd. She must either join them now, or anger them and risk the consequences. She glanced at Rhys. He smiled encouragingly.

He didn't *look* crazy. And he *had* promised to keep her safe....

She trusted him. It was totally irrational, but she did.

So with a deep breath, she rose to her feet, held her head high and walked through the magnificent silver double doors of the Great Western Gate. And hoped to hell she hadn't just sealed her fate.

Seth-Aziz held out his hands to her as she crossed the threshold. "Welcome home, my dear Gillian."

Whatever fate that might be…

Chapter 11

I dream lying dreams of your love lost,
And my heart stands still inside me.
— Song of the Birdcatcher's Daughter

Rhys felt like a bastard. There were no two ways about it—he'd misled Gillian, gotten her here under somewhat false pretenses. Which in itself was nothing new. But feeling like a bastard about it was.

He did not like that feeling one bit.

But did he have a choice? No. He was fulfilling his duties as master steward of Khepesh, something he'd done countless times before. So what was different about this time?

Foolish question.

Gillian. The fact that he desperately wanted her for himself.

That had never happened before.

As he watched Seth take possession of her, he had to physically restrain himself from stepping between them. Luckily, Nephtys did it in his place.

"My lord, allow me to take Gillian to the temple. The ceremony is in five short days. She must be quickly taught our ways and prepared."

"Yes, of course," Seth said, though Rhys could tell he was loath to release his hold on her.

"I promised she'd be shown around the palace," Rhys interjected, mindful of the deer-in-headlights look she was now giving him. "So she can see how we live, and what to expect of her future here with us. I know she has many questions."

"That I'll leave in your capable hands," Seth told him, finally letting her go of hers.

"But, Rhys—" she began to protest.

He cut her off. "I'll see you tomorrow, Miss Haliday. Tonight just relax and settle in."

"But—"

"Nephtys will take good care of you. We'll talk in the morning."

Rhys smiled reassuringly at her as the priestess led her away, already calculating what excuse he could concoct to break protocol tonight and see her.

The crowd dispersed, and he and Seth set off for the council chambers, where they were to meet with the rest of Khepesh's leaders to update the plans for the ceremony, now that the sacrificial vessel had been chosen. He must also inform Seth of Haru-Re's threat.

"She's perfect," Seth said as they strode along. "As usual you manage to exceed my expectations, Kilpatrick. I couldn't have asked for better."

"I'm glad you're pleased," Rhys returned, then cleared his throat. "There's something I'd like to discuss with you, my lord."

"*Very* pleased," Seth continued, brushing off his request. "Did you hear Nephtys had a vision of the woman?"

Rhys frowned, a tingle of foreboding trickling through his veins. "Indeed?"

"She says Miss Haliday will come to be greatly respected by the people of Khepesh. And that we will be happy together, she and I, as true lovers."

Rhys's heart nearly stopped beating. *That changed everything.* If it was true, Rhys had no chance at all to claim Gillian as his own. "Is that right? Nephtys saw this?"

"Earlier. Just before you arrived. It's why there were so many at the gate to receive you. They wanted a glimpse of the woman the god has smiled upon."

Pain and jealousy raged through Rhys, but he forced himself to say, "That's wonderful news, Seth. It's about time you found a woman of your heart." And normally Rhys would honestly be pleased for his friend. He'd been alone for a long time. But why did it have to be *this* woman?

"Yes," Seth said thoughtfully. "She is beautiful. Though she seems a bit…timid. And obviously terrified of me. I suppose that'll change in time."

"This must all be strange and overwhelming to her," Rhys said. "Give her a chance to get used to things. To you."

"There won't be much opportunity for that before the ceremony," Seth observed with a frown.

"You needn't join your flesh with hers—" Rhys swallowed "—immediately afterward."

"It's tradition."

"But not a requirement for the ritual. What you really need is the nourishment of her blood. The sex is just for added pleasure."

"I suppose so."

"If you like this woman, you should take extra care." Nearly choking on the words, Rhys added, "You'll have all eternity to enjoy the pleasures of her body."

"Very true." Seth clasped his shoulder. "Your counsel is wise, Englishman. It's unlike me to restrain myself, but I'll give it some serious thought."

"Good," Rhys said. "Meanwhile, I'll look out for her. Make sure she learns the things appropriate to the high priest's consort."

And try desperately to figure out just how in

hell he'd go about changing Seth's mind about her. Because when it came to Gillian, Rhys wasn't certain *he'd* be able to restrain himself.

But if one or the other didn't happen, immortal or not, he had a nasty feeling his days on earth were numbered.

"You mustn't be afraid. No one here is going to harm you."

Gillian met the concerned eyes of the priestess Nephtys. Lithe and petite, with a cloud of angelic copper-colored hair and a penetrating gaze, the woman was a curious mix of youthful sensuality and womanly wisdom. Her shadowed eyes held a patina of emotions that Gillian couldn't pin down. But she seemed sincere in this, at least.

"Okay," Gillian said, but sounded unconvinced even to herself.

Nephtys smiled. "It's a start. Come, let me show you where you'll be staying for now."

The rooms and halls they walked through had Gillian's jaw dropping in amazement. Burning torch-sconces lit their way, illuminating soaring columns, elaborately carved reliefs, gorgeous painted murals on the stone walls depicting scenes of the gods and secular life aboveground, luxurious tapestries and a collection of glass and precious metal objects and statuary that any museum would envy. The palace seemed to be endless. Josslyn would die and go to heaven for a glimpse of just one of these rooms.

She shoved aside thoughts of her sister. She didn't want to break down and cry. Would she ever see Joss and Gemma again?

They came to a set of silver double doors, smaller than Khepesh's monumental Western Gate but no less magnificent, which were opened by a pair of young women. They smiled genially and inclined their heads respectfully to Gillian and Nephtys as they passed through.

They entered a large, rectangular room with columns lining the walls. "This is the hypostyle hall," Nephtys said, "where people come to feast and celebrate. And this," she said as they went through the next room, "is the Courtyard of the Sacred Pool of Set-Sutekh." The room was made of forest-green marble, including a large, square raised basin, filled with sparkling water, and water lilies, their huge round-rimmed pads bearing bright pink flowers.

"Night-blooming *Victoria amazonica*," Nephtys explained at Gillian's astonished look at the unusual plants. "Rhys received the first one as a gift from Howard Carter."

She shot her a startled glance. "The Howard Carter who discovered King Tut's tomb?"

Nephtys waved a hand. "Well. On a tip from Rhys. Carter was getting too close to the eastern tomb entrance to Khepesh, so he was…offered a distraction, shall we say?"

"Sort of like I was," Gillian muttered, skipping over the whole issue of the famous archaeologist's death in 1939. All right, so she'd seen ample evidence that what Rhys had told her was all true, but she still found the notion of immortality hard to swallow.

"Not exactly," Nephtys said wryly. "Carter wasn't half as clever as you, and would never have found the entry mechanism. But he had to be dealt with in any case. Anyone coming too close is a potential danger."

"I can imagine," Gillian said, taking in her exquisite surroundings. "If this place were ever discovered, you'd have some major explaining to do."

"It won't be," Nephtys returned with an indulgent lift of her lips. "Ever." There was a wealth of information conveyed in her slight emphasis of the last word.

A shiver worked up Gillian's spine. The priestess was really subtly saying that *she* would never be found.

As though reading her mind, Nephtys said, "You'll like it here, Gillian. I promise you. I also was a captive once, and I grew to love my captor with all my heart. You will, too. You'll see."

So there it was, official now. She *was* a captive. The thought should have been more upsetting than it was. But she was strangely calm.

Because of Rhys.

What would Nephtys say if Gillian told her she was already halfway there? That despite missing her family dreadfully, the thought of spending the next thousand years with Rhys Kilpatrick made this whole situation far less terrifying? That deep down, she was even a little excited about it? Was that crazy?

"My brother may appear intimidating, but he's a good man with a wonderful heart," Nephtys assured her.

"You're Rhys's sister?" Gillian asked in surprise.

The other woman blinked. "Goodness, no. I meant Seth, of course."

"Oh. But—"

Just then they stepped through the portal to the inner sanctum, and instantly everything else fell from her mind. The sanctuary was breathtaking. Torch-lined walls were clad in glittering silver, the floor made of obsidian so black her feet seemed to be treading upon the empty void of outer space. But it was the arched ceiling that truly made her breath catch. The whole curved expanse was fashioned of dark blue lapis lazuli the exact color of the night sky, spangled with what could only be diamonds, sparkling and winking in the same constellations as the trillion stars over the real desert above.

"Beautiful, isn't it?" Nephtys said proudly.

"Beautiful doesn't come close," Gillian said in awe.

"I'm glad you like it. This is where your ceremony will take place."

The spell shattered, and her attention snapped to the series of gorgeous pedestaled altars Nephtys indicated. There were six of them, lined up on each side of an intricately carved obsidian sarcophagus that also served as a large central altar, overflowing with fragrant offerings of flowers and fruit and goblets of wine. As far as venues went, it was splendid. But Gillian had no intention of becoming a sacrificial virgin.

"Look, um, I understand this ritual is important to your, um, *per netjer,* but I really don't think I'm interested in being part of it."

Nephtys tilted her head and studied her. "Didn't Lord Kilpatrick explain everything to you?"

"Just that it involves blood, and that I must be willing."

"I see," the priestess mused. "Well, I suppose that's true…in a way."

Gillian was starting to get a bad feeling. "What are you saying?"

Nephtys walked to the sarcophagus and

ran her fingers along the smooth top. "It is a great honor to be chosen by the god. Any one of the *shemsu* of Set-Sutekh would take your place in a heartbeat. Taking mortal blood is required once a year, but immortals can be used in a pinch to tide him over. So there is really no need for an unwilling participant."

"Okay. Good." She felt a "but" coming.

"But my brother has his heart set on you."

"Oh." She also felt a buzz of warning.

"And he generally gets what he wants."

Gillian didn't miss the implication. Nor did she doubt it. The man was intimidating as hell. But surely this wasn't what it sounded like... She swallowed. "I guess I could learn more about the ritual," she hedged. "Find out what's involved. Then decide."

Again she got that indulgent little smile. "It's not complicated. I can tell you right now."

"Okay."

"It's called the Ritual of Transformation, because during the ceremony the high priest is transformed into the living embodiment of the god Set-Sutekh. But it should probably be called the Ritual of Transfusion. You see, once a year Seth must partake of fresh human blood from a female, to replenish his own. Naturally, the whole ceremony is filled with pomp and circumstance, but the actual act is quite simple. You lie upon the altar and he drinks from your neck."

Her *neck?*

Gillian froze where she stood, her eyes bugging out. "My G-god," she stammered. "Seth-Aziz... He really *is* a v-vampire?"

Nephtys seemed shocked. "Sweet Isis. I thought you knew."

"Naturally I've heard the stories, but I didn't actually believe... I never imagined... Jesus, would I become a vampire, too, after that?"

"Mercifully, no. That's just a myth," Nephtys said, and Gillian sagged with relief. "But you do gain a good measure of power. Certain skills... and pleasures. Your participation is amply rewarded."

Gillian glanced around again, her mind in a chaotic whirl. "But all this silver everywhere. Isn't silver lethal to vampires?"

Nephtys smiled. "Not here in Egypt. Nor silver bullets, wooden stakes, crosses or garlic.

None of that has any effect on Seth. Only the rays of the sun."

"But he does drink blood."

"Just once a year. And only a small quantity. It's not about hunger. It is a requirement for his continued immortality. A bargain made long ago with his goddess Sekhmet. Over the year she steals the strength of his blood, so he must replenish it or weaken and perish."

Thus the annual sacrifice. The word *sacrifice* triggered what Seth had said to Rhys as she'd entered Khepesh. *She'll make a succulent sacrifice…and a worthy consort.*

Again, alarm tingled up the back of her neck. Oh. My. God. She'd almost forgotten about that among the plethora of other panic-inducing stuff. Surely, he didn't plan to make *her* his—

"—honestly, it's not the least bit scary. Hollywood likes to overdramatize things so. And that Transylvanian upstart—" Nephtys rolled her eyes "—he really ruined it for—"

"Wait!" Gillian choked out. "Is there more?" she interrupted with growing dismay. "To the ritual? After the blood-drinking part?"

Nephtys regarded her for a long

moment. "Yes," she said at length. "Sometimes there is."

"What happens?" she demanded.

"If the god wills it, the sacrificial vessel is bestowed a great honor," Nephtys said, her eyes redolent with secret knowledge.

Gillian swallowed heavily. "And what is that?" she asked in a hoarse whisper. "Tell me."

"The most holy act of all. The god takes her body to his," the priestess said softly. "And joins his flesh with hers as one."

Chapter 12

Oh, throw the temple gates of her wide,
his mistress readies for sacrifice!
—Nakht Sobek, scribe in the City of the
Dead

At Khepesh, palace intrigues were, on the whole, a thing of the past. Seth strove to maintain harmony and worked hard to see that everyone was happy and content in their lives as the immortals of Set-Sutekh. Which was why palace guards were found solely at the outside gates and aboveground, all under the command of Sheikh Shahin Aswadi.

In other words, there were no inconvenient guards to hinder Rhys's progress into the temple compound that night. And he would have been very surprised if Nephtys had posted a sentinel at Gillian's door. After all, where could she go?

Obviously, Nephtys did not know Gillian at all.

And Gillian didn't know Khepesh. Being underground with no difference between night and day, people would be about at all hours. Including the men guarding the palace exits.

Which was why Rhys had decided to post himself in the Courtyard of the Sacred Pool, just outside the entrance to the *haram* of the temple priestess and *shemat*s, where Gillian had been given rooms. He had little doubt she'd appear before the night was through.

He'd extinguished all but one of the everburning sconces, and stretched out on the wide-rimmed lip of the sacred basin, hands stacked under his head, hoping the pineapple-and-spice scent of the water lilies and tinkling sound of the cascading water would soothe his frayed nerves and soothe his rattled composure.

He desperately needed to speak with Gillian. To explain. To beg her to—what? There was precious little either of them could do at this point to change what was happening.

Hell, he really just wanted to see her.

He'd nearly fallen into an uneasy slumber when, sure enough, she slipped out through the *haram* door, candle in hand.

"Going somewhere?" he asked with voice low, annoyance joining his unaccustomed jumble of emotions. Sometimes he really hated being right.

She gasped, whirling to face him so quickly her candle flew from her hand, its flame out in an instant, leaving them in near darkness. "Rhys?"

He rose lithely to his feet. "Did Nephtys not tell you the consequences of trying to escape?"

"Yes!" she hissed angrily. "She said I'd be robbed of my personality and will, left to live as a zombie forever. Something *you* failed to mention."

"I'm sorry, Gillian." He approached and

grasped her nearly bare shoulders. She was still wearing the delicate gown he'd given her that morning. *A good sign.* "I had no choice but to bring you here. You set that in motion yourself. And believe me, you would have liked the alternative even less."

She shook him off. "You *lied* to me!"

"No, I didn't lie. But admittedly, I did leave out some details."

"No shit." She spun on a toe and stalked toward the courtyard portal that glowed like a beacon in the darkness. "I am so outta here."

He caught her arm. "You'd rather be a zombie, as you call it, than—"

"Than become a sex slave and blood donor to a freaking *vampire* for all eternity? Ya *think?* Rhys, he plans to *rape* me at this so-called ceremony!" She wrenched free again and continued striding toward the temple exit.

"He's *not* going to rape you, Gillian. If that part happens at all, the woman must be willing."

"Tell that to Nephtys. She seems to think it's already decided!"

He took a second to gather his powers. He'd

been in such personal turmoil he'd been acting like a mortal. He quickly sent out a spell blocking the portal with an invisible force field.

She ran into it, narrowed her eyes at the solid air and pounded at it with a furious fist. "Damn it! Let me *go,* Rhys."

"Hell, no. You are going to listen to me."

She banded her arms across her chest, but didn't turn. Her gossamer dress fluttered in the wave of his impatience. "Why would I listen to a goddamn word you say? *Nothing* you say has been true." Her voice hitched.

"You're wrong," he said, grasping her shoulders again. "I meant every word I said."

"Liar!"

He pulled her stiff frame backward against his chest and wrapped his arms around her from behind. He felt her heart rhythm leap. But she didn't struggle against him. So he let his hands smooth slowly down the sensual dips and curves of her body. His own flesh quickened and his breath came faster.

"Bodies don't lie," he murmured. "Neither yours nor mine. We ache to be lovers, and I swear to you, I'll do everything in my power to see that Seth does not take you as his consort or put more than teeth to you at the ceremony."

She jetted out a breath. "What chance is there that you'll succeed? He seems...determined. And what about what Nephtys said? About that vision she had? She claims I'll be *happy* as his consort in the future." She turned in his arms. "But I really don't see that happening, unless I've been completely robbed of my will, so there you go. Zombieland, here I come."

Despite the contradiction, he felt compelled to defend his friend. "I promise, he hasn't taken a woman yet who didn't want him. He's a vampire, darling, not a monster."

Her shoulders notched down a bit. "Truthfully, he doesn't seem like such a bad guy. I just can't see myself ever falling in love with him."

Immeasurable relief flooded through Rhys. When had it become so important to him that she return his overwhelming desire in equal measure? Though he hadn't admitted it to himself until this moment, he'd been terrified that under the circumstances she might shift her affections to Seth.

"You just met the man," he forced himself

to say. "How can you know your feelings with such certainty? Most women find Seth impossible to resist."

She let out a long sigh. Then laid her cheek against his chest and whispered, "I know…because I'm already falling for someone else."

Gillian's heart pounded painfully, waiting for Rhys to react to her unexpected declaration. At length his arms tightened around her and he murmured, "We are both in such deep trouble."

The understatement of the millennium, if her take on the situation was anywhere near accurate.

"What do we do?" she asked, finally letting herself sink into his embrace. He hadn't exactly returned her sentiment, but at least he'd included himself in his equation of doom. Did that mean he felt something for her, as well? Beyond his obvious lust? Her head was spinning with everything that had been thrown at her over the past twenty-four hours. She was so far out of her field of experience she was in a whole other universe. Literally. "How can we hope to change Seth's mind if he believes Nephtys's vision of the future is correct?"

"Nephtys has rarely been known to be wrong," Rhys said. "But it does happen. The future is not set in stone. Its course can shift an infinite number of ways, taking everyone by surprise. She knows that. So does Seth. I'll just have to convince them this is one of those times."

"Do you think it'll work?" she murmured.

"It has to."

His lips swept over hers and a wisp of need spun through her center. "Oh, Rhys, what will we do if he won't let me go?"

"Shh. Don't think that way." His mouth covered hers and his fingers bunched in her dress.

She moaned as he kissed her slowly, thoroughly, the wet, languorous explorations of his tongue turning her brain to mush. She fell backward against the solid wall of nothingness that he'd conjured to block the portal, and it turned soft, like a body, enveloping her backside in a warm, living cushion.

Desire spilled through her, filling her flesh with a dazzling need for him, lighting her skin with breathless sensitivity to his touch. He slowly caressed her, awakening every cell of her body. She felt herself spinning out of control. Wanting him. Needing this. She'd never felt this way before, so turned on and ready for a man, her blood heavy and her muscles leaden.

"Are you bespelling me?" she groaned between kisses.

"It is you who have bespelled me," he returned, kissing her harder, more greedily. More urgently.

She answered with a moan, fumbling with his clothes to find a way in. She wanted to touch his bare skin.

But he found hers first. He slid the straps of her filmy gown off her shoulders, and it slithered down the length of her body to the floor, leaving her naked.

He muttered a strangled oath, and swept her up into his arms. "I must have you. Now."

"What if they find out?" she asked, terrified of the answer.

"I don't care. You belong to *me*. Nothing can change that."

She clung to him as he turned, hesitated, then

strode into the hidden inner sanctum, the holy of holies where the seven altars stood laden with Khepesh's gifts to the god.

He swept aside the offerings from the center altar, the lid of Seth's large obsidian sarcophagus, and laid her upon it. She sucked in a breath, looking downward askance. "He's not sleeping in it now, is he?"

"Christ, no. That only happens once a month during the full moon," he assured her.

Two torches still burned in the sanctuary, and she could see his face in the flickering firelight. His cheek muscles were drawn, his black mustache a slash of determination above the tight line of his lips, his amber eyes half-lidded and darkened to the color of fine whiskey. He was wearing a finely woven tunic tucked into black Bedouin pants, and looked so sinfully sexy she didn't know what to do with herself.

"Are you sure about this?" she asked shakily, not sure if she'd let him stop even if he wanted to.

He drew off his tunic and boots and threw them aside. "If your body is to be a gift to Set-Sutekh," he said with a low growl, "it is

I who will bestow it. And if our love is to be sacrificed, what better place to offer it up than here?"

"But Rhys—"

He climbed up on the altar and positioned his body over hers. "Do you want me? Do you want me above all else, no matter what may come of it?"

Gillian swallowed, torn as never before. She might be new to this place, but even she knew that by doing this they could well be putting their lives at risk. Seth didn't seem the forgiving type.

But she wanted Rhys. Oh, how she wanted him! She wanted to lie under him, joined as one, and be swallowed up by the strength and power that rolled off him like liquid waves of sand and filled her with raw desire. She wanted him to touch her, and know her, and shower her with forbidden pleasures. She wanted to come apart in his arms, and drown in the feeling of belonging that she had experienced only with him.

"Yes," she said. "I want you, Rhys. No matter what."

His mouth came down on hers and his chest scraped over her breasts, sending shards of need spiraling through her nipples. She gasped, opening to his ravenous kiss.

In the courtyard he'd been languid, gentle; now he was forceful and demanding. His hands and lips traveled her body, raising moans and cries of pleasure from her aching throat.

She surrendered to it. To him.

What would be, would be. *This* was right. She knew it in her heart.

He moved down and took her breasts in his mouth, suckling and giving them small bites, driving her mad for want of him. He put his knee between her legs and spread them, cupping her mound, sliding his fingers through the slick folds and finding the center of her need.

He touched her there.

It was like an atom bomb of pleasure went off in her body. She cried out and bowed up, her orgasm coming fast and hard.

He growled and touched her again, and another shock of pleasure shook her to the core. She was panting, her pulse racing, her flesh saturated with a thousand intense feelings and sensations all at once.

He grasped her hands and pulled them above her head, lacing his fingers with hers, pinning her to the cool, smooth obsidian surface. He levered his body over hers and she realized he was now as naked as she.

And then he was inside her.

Thick and long and burning hot, his cock thrust in deep, deep, deep. He withdrew and thrust again, and again, and again. She wanted to scream in pleasure but couldn't find her voice. She shook and shuddered as his awesome power showered over her like an endless, thundering electrical storm, seemingly forever, until at last he gave one final forceful thrust and with a roar he came apart in her arms.

They lay there, bodies one and hearts galloping, for a long while, regaining their breath, recovering their limbs, coming slowly back to consciousness of the world around them.

All was quiet and calm.

All except inside Gillian's mind. There reigned nothing but chaos.

Not just because what they'd done would

surely get them into massive trouble—if not worse—but because of the overwhelming feelings she was starting to have for Rhys.

How could she be so much in love with a man she'd just met? He claimed he hadn't used magic on her, but how else could she explain such an instant bond? Love at first sight? She could just imagine what Josslyn would have to say about *that*. Oy.

Gemma, though. Gemma would probably just smile, give her a hug and tell her to elope with the man.

"You okay?" Rhys asked softly, giving her a tender kiss, bringing her back to the moment.

"More than okay," she murmured, brushing aside wistful thoughts of missing her sisters. She returned his kiss, stretching her pleasantly aching muscles. "You are amazing."

"And you are inspiring." He kissed her back.

She smiled, but it soon faltered and she closed her eyes, unable to banish her worry completely. "Oh, Rhys, what happens now? There's no way I can go through with that ceremony. And as for being his consort—never in a million years."

With a sigh, he lifted off her and helped her

sit up. "For now, we go on as though nothing has changed. We still have a few days. Let me work on Seth. He's firm but not unreasonable. Maybe I can find a substitute." He winked. "Another blonde, so he doesn't miss you."

She looked at him aghast. "Rhys, no! You can't kidnap another innocent woman!"

He held up a hand. "Rarely do we resort to kidnapping, Gillian. Only when we are some-how threatened. Most of the *shemsu* come to us by choice." He reached out and scraped a lock of hair from her cheek. "What about your sisters? One of them is a blonde, as I recall. Would she not like to live forever? Or we could just borrow her for the night. She would remember nothing…."

Gillian felt her eyes widen. "Don't you *dare!*"

"Very well. I just thought you might miss them."

"I do." She put her hand over his. "More than you know. But I couldn't ask this of either one of them. It wouldn't be fair to trade my unhappiness for theirs."

He gathered her in his arms, rested his chin on her hair. "Are you so unhappy here, then?"

She burrowed deeper into his embrace. "Not while I'm with you, Rhys. But I'm terrified of what will happen if Seth-Aziz doesn't change his mind about me."

"Leave it to me, my love. For now you must return to your rooms before you are missed. I'll come fetch you in the morning for your palace tour as planned. We'll talk more then."

But when he moved to go, she held him tight. Apparently, he didn't want to leave any more than she did, because he leaned down and kissed her with a fervor that was almost frightening. Her response was just as desperate.

They made love again, with an intensity that drove the danger from their minds for a few more precious minutes, until they were both drained of strength and breath...and caution.

Which was why, when they finally parted at the *haram* door, neither of them saw the hidden figure hovering in the darkest corner of the courtyard. Observing their lingering kiss goodbye.

Chapter 13

But if someone would say, "There's a lady
here, waiting,"
Hear that, and you'd see me take heart in
a hurry!

—Papyrus Chester Beatty I

Nephtys stood in the shadows and watched
the lovers kiss and reluctantly go their separate
ways.

A small part of her felt sorry for them. She, of
all people, knew so well that one did not choose
with whom one fell in love. It just happened.

And usually at the most heartbreakingly inappropriate of times, with the least suitable person possible.

But mostly she felt anger and outrage. On behalf of her brother, who had been cuckolded right under his nose. And on behalf of Khepesh, which would no doubt suffer unforeseen consequences because of this betrayal. Gillian was to have been a wise and well-loved consort. Rhys was a valued member of the council as well as an insightful adviser to Seth-Aziz. He would be sorely missed when he was banished for his disloyalty.

Troubled, Nephtys stepped out from the shadows and made her way back to her suite in the *haram*. There was no option. She must report this treachery to her brother.

But first she should seek her own counsel. The Eye of Horus. Perhaps another vision would guide her in how best to handle this situation.

She made haste to the prayer room, where she kept the scrying bowl in its place of honor on a golden pedestal. Silver was the color of the moon, and therefore the sacred metal of Khepesh, palace of the Guardian of the Night;

but the amber bowl was hewn for and named after the god of their enemy, Re-Horakhti, Lord of the Sun, and therefore would be offended by a resting place of anything but the finest yellow gold.

She lifted the bowl and brought it to her favorite spot for meditation, amidst a scatter of soft cushions surrounded by a hundred ever-burning, delicately fragrant candles. She gingerly lifted a two-thousand-year-old Roman glass pitcher that had been filled with water smuggled to her by a spy she maintained in the temple of her own betrayer and Seth's immortal nemesis, Haru-Re.

"Bring me a vision of wisdom, oh, Eye of Horus," she prayed as she poured the sacred water into its depths. "So I may best know what to do."

But when the vision came, sudden and vivid like a dust storm surging to life in the desert, her hand convulsed around the fragile glass pitcher and it shattered in a million pieces. Blood dripped from a dozen cuts on her fingers, turning the whirling waters scarlet. But she barely noticed.

She gasped in dismay at what she saw.

Haru-Re was standing in his palace audience chamber, lifting his arms in welcome to a new immortal follower of Re-Horakhti.

It was *Rhys Kilpatrick*.

"Something's wrong. I can feel it."

At Gillian's hushed but urgently spoken words, Rhys glanced around to make sure they were alone. As promised, he'd picked her up in the temple right after the morning meal, ostensibly to show her the rest of the palace, introduce her to her new way of life and outline the duties expected of her. He'd spent the hours before breakfast locked in the council chambers together with Seth and the others, planning strategies to deal with the ultimatum Haru-Re had laid down yesterday when he'd appeared at Rhys's house—either hand over Nephtys or go to war. There had been no opportunity to talk to Seth about any other issue.

"Nephtys knows," Gillian said now as they strolled through the palace pretending to look at the magnificent sights it offered. "I know she does."

"Darling, what makes you say that?" he asked.

She frowned worriedly. "She wouldn't look at me the whole time we ate, and she barely spoke to me all morning. Plotting my sacrifice, no doubt. Except in *this* ceremony I don't survive to become consort."

He winced. She had no idea how right on the mark she could be if their guilty secret were revealed. Which was why the two of them must not make love again. Not until Seth had given his blessing. "I'm sure Nephtys is just worried about Haru-Re's threat," he said. "I understand there's some history there. I've heard her say she'd rather give up eternal life altogether than go back to serve him."

Gillian blinked. "You can do that? Give up immortality?"

"Well, quasi-immortality. Don't forget, we *can* be killed if certain methods are employed." A thought uppermost in his mind that morning. Seth was not a violent man by nature, but even he had his limits. "Otherwise immortality is all a matter of maintenance." He didn't like thinking about the tenuousness of their state of being, either. Too many things could go awry—as evidenced by the fact that Khepesh and Petru were the last two remaining of the thousands of ancient *per netjer* that had once flourished in Egypt. "If the ceremonies are not performed and the correct incantations not recited in a timely fashion, the magic simply fades away. Eventually you become mortal again, and pick up where you left off. More or less."

She blinked again. "Wow. Seriously?"

"That's why banishment from Khepesh is… undesirable."

"Yeah. I get that."

"Of course, being drained completely of one's blood by an angry vampire is probably a worse fate," he muttered.

Her jaw dropped in horror. *"What?"*

Oops. Had he said that aloud?

She covered her eyes with unsteady fingers. "Please tell me you're kidding."

He forced a smile and tapped the end of her nose. "Don't worry, he hasn't done that in nearly a millennium. And he did it only to someone who'd deserted to the enemy camp, a traitor to the god. Seth had no choice but to avenge the insult."

She dropped her fingers. "What about an insult to him personally? Oh, Rhys, we are so screwed."

"Have a little faith," he told her. "This thing with Haru-Re may provide the means to distract him."

"Dear God, I hope so."

They'd arrived in a huge, three-story room canted by galleries and filled floor-to-ceiling with rows and rows of bookshelves. Some contained books, some files of papers, some ancient papyrus rolls. Several wooden tables were scattered throughout the room and galleries, with a handful of people reading or studying at them.

Gillian looked at it all in astonishment. "Is this what I think it is?" she asked.

"Five thousand years worth of historical documentation," he affirmed, recalling that she was a student of history. "The most complete library of its kind in existence. Other than the one maintained by Haru-Re at Petru."

To his surprise, her eyes became misty. "Oh,

my God," she whispered. "Do you have any idea how incredible this is?"

"A bit."

Moved by her sincere reaction, he wanted to take her into his arms and kiss her forehead, acknowledge her wonderstruck awe at the discovery of such historical bounty. But the eyes of everyone in the room had lifted and were on them. He crossed his arms. "One can lose oneself for decades and not even scratch the surface. Believe me, I've done it."

She dabbed the corner of her eye with an embarrassed laugh. "Well, at least I'll never be bored living here."

"That," he said, "is a certainty." He paused. "But today I thought we'd take a look at one particular book."

She gave him a curious look as he led her deep into the stacks to a section that dealt with everything known about Petru, the palace of Haru-Re. He pulled out a thick, heavy, parchment book and laid it on a nearby table.

"What is this?" she asked as he carefully opened it, revealing handwritten pages containing lists of names and dates.

He found the last entry and started to leaf back from there. "It is a register of Petru's initiates—the ones we know of—and the approximate dates they were admitted to the *per netjer* of Re-Horakhti." He looked gravely at her. "When did you say your mother disappeared?"

She stared at him, the terrible understanding slowly twisting her face. "You think she was taken captive by Haru-Re?"

"I don't know," he answered truthfully. "Ray hasn't usually taken captives, either, unless desperate. It's too risky. But in that photo you found, the man with your mother was one of his most trusted lieutenants. Why would she be with him if she hadn't joined the *per netjer?*"

Gillian's troubled gaze went to the book. "Nineteen ninety," she told him. "But if she went to Petru, it was not willingly. She would never have left our family."

"Let's see if she's even listed." He ran his finger down the handful of entries for the correct year. "Our information is not always complete."

But Gillian was way ahead of him. She let out a soft cry and put a shaking finger on the page. "Oh, my God! Her name *is* here!" She looked up at him in dismay. "Oh, Rhys, my mother is being held by that madman!"

Gillian could barely breathe. "I must go to her!" She leaped up, intending to run.

Rhys's strong grip on her arm held her in place, an immovable restraint. "Not an option."

She struggled against his control. "But they're keeping her against her will! We have to rescue her!"

"Darling, stop." He glanced around. They were attracting even more attention now. "Let's go somewhere where we can talk."

"There's nothing to talk about," she insisted as he tugged her through the library and out into the grand hallway. But they still weren't alone. "My mother *needs* me."

He kept walking, and turned down an unfamiliar but deserted corridor. "Are you sure about that?"

"Of course I am. What are you suggesting?"

They'd entered what seemed to be a quiet residential wing. He remained silent until after they'd arrived at a patterned silver door, he'd opened it and hustled her inside. "Gillian, what if she *chose* to join the *per netjer* of Re-Horakhti?"

"I've told you before. She wouldn't have."

"All right, fine. Say that's true, and for argument's sake, let's also say by some miracle you are able to escape Khepesh without bringing down the wrath of the high priest upon yourself. So you show up at the doorstep of Petru and—" he put his palm to his forehead "—except, oh, wait, you have no idea where it is."

Hurt brushed along the fringes of her heart. "But *you* do. You could tell me. You could *show* me."

His lips thinned. "Do you have any idea what Haru-Re would *do* to you?"

Nothing pleasant, she knew, because he'd intimated as much yesterday when they'd met at Rhys's house. "Not if you're with me," she reasoned.

His gaze was even. "Now you want me to betray Seth?"

"You already have," she reminded him.

A muscle twitched in his cheek. "Yes, and he's been my best friend for a hundred twenty-five years. What makes you think your mother any less perfidious than I?"

"I just know it," she said unhappily, and turned away to escape his angry regard. She suddenly noticed they were standing in the drawing room of a private residence. It was furnished much like the one in Rhys's house aboveground. "Are these your apartments?" she asked in surprise.

"Yes," he said.

"Is that wise? Should we even be here?" she asked.

"Hell, no. But I couldn't have you talking treason out in the open hallways. Remember what I said happened to the last person who defected to the enemy?"

A twist of fear wound through her. "What am I supposed to do then? What if they've turned my mother into a zombie because she wouldn't join willingly? Do I just—"

"*Shabti,*" he interrupted, his mouth turned down in distaste.

"What?"

"We call them *shabtis,* human servants, not

zombies. That implies death, and they are very much alive."

"In body, anyway. You saw her face in the photo, Rhys. Did she look like a normal, happy woman to you?"

He pushed out a breath. "It was a split second in time, Gillian. Maybe her shoes were pinching her."

She scowled. "You don't really believe that."

"Even if I don't, there's nothing we can do to help her. Not from here. Not right now." He sighed. "Perhaps in time we can arrange a trade."

"In *time?*"

"Darling, remember your own current position here at Khepesh is tenuous at best. Until things are…decided, you shouldn't rock the boat with talk of haring off to Petru." His tone carried more than a shade of rebuke.

She squeezed her eyes shut, feeling the hot sting of tears behind the lids. She knew he was right. But that didn't make it any easier to ignore the sick feeling in the pit of her stomach.

With a curse, he opened his arms. "By the stars. Come here."

She went into them gratefully, needing the comfort of his nearness. He lowered his lips to hers, and she met them, shuddering out a sigh of need, holding him close.

Her body recognized him immediately as her lover, the man who'd spent hours last night worshipping her with untold pleasures. She wanted that feeling back again. The emotional closeness. The incredible sense of belonging. She opened to him, inviting him in. Their mouths melded in a drowning kiss.

Swearing an oath, a few seconds later Rhys tore his lips from hers and stepped back. "No, my love. We mustn't do this. Not until I've spoken with Seth."

"And that, my friend," came a rough and angry male voice from behind her, "is the first intelligent thing I've heard you utter."

Chapter 14

Let not my heart be fashioned anew
according to all the evil things said
against me.

—*The Book of the Dead*

Sheikh Shahin Aswadi stood in the wide
passage to Rhys's kitchen, brandishing his
scimitar.

Gillian spun around and let out a cry of fear
as Rhys froze in shock. He reached out and
tucked her protectively behind his back.

"What are you doing here?" he asked his

friend—hell, he hoped Shahin was still his friend after what the man had just witnessed.

"Trying to save your pathetic hide," Shahin responded with a look of fury and disgust. "When Nephtys told me what you were up to with this woman, I didn't want to believe her. I had to see for myself that you are a traitor."

"I am no traitor," Rhys growled. He planted his fists on his hips. "Yesterday at my house you saw how things were between us. You made no such accusations then."

"Because it wasn't the first time you'd used sex to entice a female to become Seth's sacrifice," Shahin reminded him pointedly. He ignored Gillian's scandalized gasp and continued with narrowed eyes. "How was I to know this one would ensnare your wits as well as your cock?"

"She has not," Rhys snapped. "I simply wish her for myself. I deserve my choice of bedmate after playing pied piper to our master for so long."

This time Gillian's gasp was of outrage. She jerked away from his protective shield. "Ex*cuse* me?"

Shahin's gaze strayed to her. "It seems the lady has a different perception of your relationship."

Rhys resisted the urge to throw a spell of oblivion over her to prevent her hearing the argument. Shahin would just reverse it. "There's nothing wrong with her perception. But I know where my duty lies. I've made her no promises I cannot keep."

She made a distressed sound, but he didn't dare turn. Shahin would not hesitate to strike.

"She spoke of seeking Petru," Shahin said, holding his weapon steady, his expression still hard with suspicion. "Why?"

"Her mother was taken by Haru-Re," Rhys said evenly. "She wants to rescue her."

Shahin's face barely registered a reaction. But Rhys saw it, swift and violent, chase through his eyes. Shahin's own family—his parents and sister—had been captured nearly three hundred years ago. And Haru-Re did not have the scruples of Seth-Aziz. Shahin's young, innocent sister had become Haru-Re's more-than-blood sacrifice, then had taken her own life rather than face the shame of her ordeal; his father had died trying to avenge her honor. His mother was still living as a *shabti* in Petru. They were the reason Shahin had joined forces with Seth-Aziz and risen to the post of commander of all the guards of Khepesh—for revenge. There was no fiercer warrior in all of Egypt than Sheikh Shahin, the legendary Black Hawk. But he never, ever spoke of his mother.

Abruptly, Shahin lowered his weapon and sheathed it. He stalked over to where Gillian stood and bent over her, nose to nose. "Forget your mother," he growled. "She is as good as dead to the world."

"Shahin!" Rhys admonished sharply. But it was too late. Gillian slapped her hands over her mouth and burst into tears. He pushed Shahin aside and reached out to comfort her, but she shrank away.

"Don't touch me!" she cried, and ran for the door.

He went to give chase, but Shahin stepped in front of him. "Let her go. She won't get far."

"That was cruel. And unnecessary." He slashed his fingers through his hair. "And now she doesn't trust me."

"As well she shouldn't. Your promises are like dust in the wind, my friend. You forget to whom she belongs."

"Her heart belongs to me. And I aim to keep the rest of her, as well."

Shahin paced away from him. "Don't be a fool! You've heard the vision of her future Nephtys has received. This woman is not for you!" He looked like he wanted to say more, but just shook his head. "Forget her, Rhys. She'll bring you only pain and dishonor, but Seth needs her."

His gut wrenched. Jealousy surged through his body, crushing his heart in a vise. "Nephtys is wrong! Gillian loves me. She'll never accept Seth as her true lover."

"Never is a long time, my friend."

Christ. He thought of eternity stretched out endlessly before him, without Gillian at his side, forced to see her living with Seth, kissing him, making love to him….

"No!" he gritted out. "No. Seth is my friend. He'll understand my feelings for her."

"Will he?" Shahin retorted. "How many lovers and consorts has he gone through under your stewardship? And when they passed, how many did he mourn for more than a few months? Do you really think he'll credit you with any deeper sentiment?"

"Then he'll surely honor Gillian's."

Shahin laughed. "Seth-Aziz is a demigod, an immortal vampire who rules his kingdom with an iron hand. Do not deceive yourself that he cares a whit for the feelings of a girl."

"You make him sound heartless."

"No. Just prudent when it comes to useless emotions. And you, Rhys, have been an unflagging moral compass against unwilling victims for these past hundred years. But you were always careful to stay aloof, even from your most eager of charges. Frankly, I'm surprised you've let yourself fall under the spell of any woman."

"This is no spell, my friend. Gillian is different."

"How so? Does she not have satin skin and tempting, soft curves like all the others?" he asked contemptuously. "And does she not have the capacity for disruption and betrayal so prevalent among her sex?"

Rhys did not need to ask how Shahin had

ended up so cynical; it had been his sister's friend, his own lover, who had betrayed his family to Haru-Re for a fat purse of gold coins. The fact that Shahin himself had escaped, and that the lover had not lived past their next meeting, had not assuaged Shahin's craving for revenge. The whole fair sex had suffered his mistrust as a consequence.

"There will be no betrayal. You may trust *my* word on that," Rhys said, feeling a brief sting of guilt at his half lie. "Now, why have you really come to see me?"

The sheikh studied him for a long moment, then apparently decided to accept his sincerity. "Nephtys sent me," he said, "to fetch Miss Haliday for the welcome feast in her honor in the grand hall. I understand Seth plans to announce his intention to take her as consort."

Dismay buzzed through Rhys at the news. Apparently Seth had discarded his advice to take it slow with Gillian. "Indeed. That was quick decided."

"After Nephtys's vision, no decision was required. Merely acceptance of what is written."

Rhys clamped his jaw. "You're saying my losing her is God's will?"

Shahin shrugged. "God, gods. Fate. The universe. Call it what you like, Englishman. Our paths are decided long before we are born."

"So you say." It was a discussion they'd had many times before, and never come to agreement. "I believe we humans have more self-determination than that," Rhys stated.

"A dangerous notion, my friend."

"Not if one's life is to have any meaning."

Shahin's face relaxed, not quite in a smile, but almost. "Life's meaning lies in following one's path with honor."

Well. It all depended on what one saw as one's path, didn't it? "No matter the obstacles?" Rhys asked tightly as they left his rooms and headed toward the grand hall.

"And to the bitter end," Shahin confirmed, grasping his shoulder and giving it a brotherly squeeze.

"Well," Rhys allowed, "on that, at least, we can agree."

As far as Rhys was concerned, his path led straight to Gillian. And one way or another, he planned to follow that path regardless of the dangers. Provided he lived long enough…

They rounded a corner and he spotted her being escorted by Nephtys's two *shemat*s back to the temple to be prepared for the feast. He took a stride toward them, but felt Shahin's hand on his shoulder again, this time heavier.

"Take care, my friend," Shahin warned. "Don't do anything you'll regret."

He ground his jaw and forced himself to halt. "What specifically did Nephtys say about us? To make you think I'm a traitor?" he asked. Shahin was silent for a heartbeat too long, and he uttered a curse. "Another of her damned prophecies?"

"Yes," Shahin said. "As well as a vision of the more…earthly variety."

Rhys darted him a stunned look. "What?"

"She saw the two of you."

"Where? At the temple?"

Shahin's eyebrows shot up. "You took her in the *temple?*" He barked out a laugh. "You are not shy about your heresy, Lord Kilpatrick."

"Seth isn't the only one who can honor the god with his sacrifice," he muttered defensively.

His friend shook his head with a pitying grin. "Ah, Rhys. I shall miss you greatly when you've been drained of your lifeblood."

"Thanks," he said drily. "But I'm not dead yet. Did she tell Seth about us?"

"I know not."

"In that case, come. Let us find our lord and master. It is time to put this matter to rest once and for all."

Rhys ducked back into his suite and quickly changed into his formal robes, spun of the finest midnight-blue silk, shot through with silver threads. He might as well look his best when he presented his case to the high priest.

He and Shahin cut splendid figures as they strode to the festival hall, he in his blue and Shahin in robes of bloodred, drawing the eye of every female they passed. It suddenly occurred to him to wonder why neither of them had chosen women to settle down with before now. Shahin was easily explained; he did not trust women further than the bedroom—preferably hers. But what of Rhys himself?

Rhys had never wanted for female companionship. But none of the women he'd known over the years had captured his interest or imagination the way Gillian did. He wasn't sure why, either. She was beautiful but not overly so, intelligent but no genius, capable and brave but not above fear of the unknown. Perhaps what spoke to him was her loyalty to her family, or the look of adoration in her eyes when their gazes met, or the way she held him tight when they embraced.

She loved him. And he loved her.

Maybe it was just as simple as that.

Except it *wasn't* simple. Because right now she belonged to another. Someone Rhys owed *his* loyalty to, and must choose before her if it came down to one or the other.

A choice that would kill him either way.

They found Seth in his private dressing room behind the grand hall, cared for as always by his sister as well as a half dozen attendants.

Rhys and Shahin bowed in greeting. "My lord."

"Ah! Just the two men I wanted to see," Seth said, shooing away the attendants. "Rhys—" he beckoned him closer as though to put an arm around his shoulders "—Nephtys tells me she has had a vision of you being welcomed with open arms at Petru."

Rhys halted in shock, his back going rigid. *"What?"* He glanced behind him at Shahin, who was standing at the ready with his hand on the hilt of his scimitar. *"Et tu, brute?"* Rhys ground out, realizing he'd been set up.

Seth waved am impatient hand. "It got me thinking that it might not be such a bad idea. To deal with this latest ultimatum of Haru-Re's, I mean. Sekhmet's blood, he's tried for ages to recruit you, Rhys. So why not let him? What do you think?"

Rhys swallowed, still uneasy. This was clearly a trap. "Surely, you don't think I would ever betray Khepesh."

"By Osiris's member, no," Seth reassured him. "I do not doubt your loyalty. But—"

"I'm glad of that," Rhys broke in, "because there is something else Nephtys has certainly brought up, which I've tried to speak with you about. It cannot wait any longer."

Seth cut him a level look, obviously annoyed at the change of topic. "This is about the woman, I assume."

"Gillian, yes," Rhys said. "I—"

"I'm sorry. You can't have her." Seth adjusted his formal headdress in front of a silver-framed mirror. "Normally I wouldn't mind stepping aside after the transformation ceremony, but Nephtys's vision of our future—"

"Is wrong," Rhys cut in emphatically. "Or it means something other than it appears to mean."

Seth turned to regard him sternly, every inch the ruling authority. "I'm sorry, Lord Kilpatrick. I don't agree. She will be my consort and that's all there is to it."

Panic seeped through Rhys's veins. He couldn't believe he was really losing her! "Miss Haliday has the highest regard for you, my lord, but she loves me. And I her. As your friend, I beg of you—"

Seth held up a hand. "This is not about my wishes or our personal friendship. You must see I've no choice but to do what is best for Khepesh. I truly am sorry."

Stunned and heartsick, Rhys followed Seth

with leaden feet as he led them into the grand hall. They took their places with the rest of the council at the head table, which sat on a raised dais at the front of the huge hall.

Once seated, Rhys swiped up his goblet of wine and drained it in a single draught, then held it up. A pretty little *shabti* appeared at his side and refilled it. As she withdrew, he put a hand on the arm that carried the carafe. "Leave it."

She bowed mutely and set it down, then padded silently away. He watched her go, and muttered to himself, "Perhaps it would not be such a terrible fate, after all, to be without a will of one's own." He drained the second goblet and reached for the carafe.

Which was when he noticed the empty chair between him and Seth. *By all the gods.* He lurched to his feet, swaying slightly, seeking someone, anyone, with whom to exchange seats.

Instead, he caught the somber gaze of his leader and best friend. "Lord Kilpatrick, take your place," Seth said in a low command.

"I cannot sit next to her as you inform

the world of her upcoming public rape," he ground out.

At Seth's other elbow, Sheikh Shahin leaped up, reaching for his weapon.

Seth shot out a hand, gesturing him back down. "Strong words, Englishman. If we weren't such good friends you would be minus your head right now."

"Perhaps it would be best that way."

"You don't mean that. Sit down. *Now*. Before I decide that you did mean it."

Rhys took a deep, steadying breath and reluctantly lowered himself back into his chair. He had to be smart about this. Shahin was right. Eternity was a long time, and losing his head was the coward's way out. Rhys's moment would come, when he could take her back, and the intervening days—or centuries—would be just an ugly splotch on their eventual happiness. He had to believe that. But in the meantime, he had to endure.

"Good," Seth said. "Now. Before I make the announcement, I want you to tell her that your feelings for her were all a ruse to get her here. That you have no personal interest in her, and wish her to go through with the full ceremony and later become my consort."

Rhys stared at the man who had been his best friend and mentor since he'd come to Khepesh, pain slicing through his heart as surely as if Shahin's sword were cleaving it in two. As of this moment, they were friends no longer.

"Very well," Rhys said, and turned his gaze upon the immortals gathering at the long rows of tables and benches that filled the grand hall to overflowing. People were laughing and hugging and making merry, because today a bright new star would be added to the galaxy of Set-Sutekh. A new initiate—the high priest's future consort, a woman who was as wise as she was beautiful.

Everyone had cause for levity and celebration.

Everyone except Rhys.

Chapter 15

Where gone, o loving man?
Why gone from her whose love
Can pace you, step by step, to your desire?
—Cairo Ostracon 25218

"You look stunning, my lady."

Gillian gazed at herself in the mirror and had to agree. The two young *shemat*s who'd dressed her must have used some kind of magical spell, because she had never looked this good before in all her days. Not even close.

"Thank you," she said, wondering if Rhys

would agree with the assessment. Not that she cared, she reminded herself.

"It's time," Nephtys told her, sweeping into the room and giving Gillian's dazzling outfit one last critical examination. A transparent film of knife-pleated, body-hugging silk in the shimmering blue-green-purple colors of abalone lay over a satin-smooth shell of delicate pink. Her breasts were high and plump in the tight, revealing bodice, her stomach flat, her legs endlessly long in the slim, floor-length gown. Except for her blond hair, she looked like a temple dancer from one of the most exquisite tomb paintings of ancient times. She supposed that was the whole idea.

"Will Rhys be there?" she asked Nephtys. Not that she cared, she reminded herself yet again. The news that he had routinely used sex to entice women to join the *per netjer* had been a shock. And his friend the sheikh—what a despicable character! How could he have said those things about her mother?

Nephtys caught her eyes in the mirror. "Yes, Lord Kilpatrick will be at the feast. Indeed, sitting next to you. But you must forget about him. He is not your destiny."

The other woman's penetrating gaze was meant to be intimidating, but she refused to back down. "I think that's for *me* to decide." She might be angry with him at the moment, but that didn't mean she wouldn't forgive him. Eventually.

"No. It's not up to you," Nephtys stated. "You have no say in the matter whatsoever. Accept that you now belong to Seth-Aziz, and things will go far easier for you."

She didn't think so. Time may have stood still here at Khepesh, but she was from the twenty-first century, where women made their own decisions. "Sorry, I can't do that."

"A shame. For it won't be you who suffers, but the man you profess to care about. If you persist in this useless infatuation, Seth will have no choice but to banish Lord Kilpatrick from Khepesh."

Gillian stared at the other woman's reflection in horror, her breath stalling in her lungs. Banishment? But that meant... "He wouldn't."

"Oh, but he would. I'm actually surprised he

hasn't yet done so, considering how far the pair of you have taken things."

Gillian's eyes widened. "How did you—"

Nephtys tutted. "Don't be naive. A blind man could see what's going on, and I am a seer. I know everything." She turned to glare at her face-to-face. "You must tell Rhys you've changed your mind about him. That you instead want the power and security being consort will bring you. Do it tonight, Gillian. Or lose him to the savage desert and the sands of time, never to be seen or heard from again."

No! Gillian felt hot, stunned tears fill her eyes. *It wasn't fair.* None of it!

She'd found Rhys Kilpatrick's grave only to lose the opportunity to inform her clients of her find; she'd found her dear lost mother alive only to lose her to mindless, hopeless captivity by a ruthless enemy; and she'd found the love of her life and a chance to be immortal only to be forced to spend eternity with a man she didn't love.

"It's not fair," she said in bleak misery.

Nephtys gave her a sad smile. "*Habibi,* who said life, even an everlasting one, is fair?"

* * *

The grand hall was amazing. It was like Gillian had been transported to the center of the Milky Way. Unlike the hypostyle hall in the temple, the interior of this festival hall was dark as the blackest night, pierced only by the sparkle of ten thousand tiny candles on the tables and, like the temple's inner sanctum, a million diamonds glittering from the ceiling overhead. Set-Sutekh was the Lord of the Night Sky, Guardian of the Dark, and this was clearly his kingdom.

But it was all lost on Gillian.

Her knees shook as she waited for the small procession to begin that would escort her down the jasmine-strewn center aisle of the room, ending at the dais where she would join the man she was to take forever as her husband. Lit up from above by the glow of magical moonbeams, Nephtys would lead, followed by Gillian, the two young *shemat*s bringing up the rear.

Almost like a wedding procession.

Gillian's heart screamed in protest over what she must do. The lie she must tell Rhys.

She could see him sitting up at the head table,

silver goblet in hand, gazing moodily out over
the room like he'd rather be anywhere but there.
Her stomach squeezed. Maybe she was wrong
about him. Maybe he didn't return her feelings.
Maybe it *had* been all about the sex and he was
glad to be rid of her, happy to go back to his
task of seducing innocent women for the sake
of the *per netjer*, relieved to leave her to the tender loving care of his vampire lord.

No! She mustn't think that way. It wasn't
true!

Oh, what did it matter, anyway? Better he not
care, so he'd be spared this howling pain that
ate at the core of her own being at the thought
of losing him.

Chords of strange, ethereal music started to
play. Nephtys nodded and stepped forward, and
Gillian floated down the aisle after her, fiercely
holding back her tears. She would *not* cry. If
she did, Rhys would never believe her change
of heart. Which he must believe at all costs. She
would *not* be responsible for his banishment and
death.

The speech of welcome Seth made to her
barely registered in her consciousness; nor

did the crowd's applause, nor her ascent to the dais and his kiss on her cheek. She did shiver though, briefly, thinking of the fangs that lay tucked behind his smiling lips, and the bloody ordeal that awaited her all too soon. To be fair, the man seemed nice. Certainly, he was handsome. And he was being extraordinarily polite and solicitous. Not to mention damn forgiving… if he knew about her and Rhys, as Nephtys had hinted.

He must have noticed the trembling of her fingers on his arm as he helped her to her seat. He cocked his head. "Are you afraid of me?"

"Yes," she admitted. "Nothing personal," she quickly added. "I'm just not used to being around…demigods and vampire priests."

"Nor being forced to marry one," he ventured, though judging by his matter-of-fact tone, the idea didn't seem to make a dent of guilt in his conscience.

"Right," she said, sitting down nervously in a bejeweled silver throne next to him. "That, too."

"You do know," he said conversationally,

"that being with me will bring you incredible physical pleasure?"

She didn't even want to *think* about that part of things. "Nephtys mentioned it."

"And you're not the least bit…curious?"

She let out a breath. "Honestly? I'd prefer to remain blissfully ignorant."

He smiled teasingly. "That will change. I have yet to receive a complaint from any woman I've touched."

Who would dare? "Unwilling pleasure is still unwilling, even if it feels good," she pointed out. Possibly foolishly.

The smile disappeared and his eyes went cold. "Now you sound like Lord Kilpatrick."

She was treading in dangerous waters, but she couldn't help herself. "Ever think he might be right?"

"No." Seth drew himself up to his full, impressive height. Even seated, he commanded uncompromising authority. "This is how things have been done for five thousand years, and so they shall remain," he decreed.

"But wouldn't you be happier spending the

next five thousand years with a woman who truly loves you?" she persisted.

"Love?" Seth gazed out at the tables filled with his joyful, celebrating subjects. "Love does not enter into it. I am the god's high priest and leader of my people. Earthly concerns and pleasures are fleeting, but my duty is enduring. Nothing else matters."

Wow. "That sounds fun," she said under her breath. She met his gaze. "And where do I fit into all this?"

He looked down at her, unmoved, and said without hesitation, "Duty."

She didn't know whether to feel sorry for him—and herself—or vastly relieved.

But all her concerns fell away into a void of oblivion when she turned to find Lord Rhys Kilpatrick sitting next to her, an intense glower marring the features of his face.

And she recalled with a painful start what she'd been told to do, and the dire consequences that he would suffer if she didn't comply.

Slowly, deliberately and a bit unsteadily, Rhys rose to his feet and raised his goblet in a toast he hoped would not appear too mocking. "My lady, I for one hope you shall be very happy in this union," he slurred, then dropped back into his seat, turned his head away and proceeded to ignore her for the rest of the festivities.

At least that was the plan. But he had little success.

Rhys found himself eavesdropping on every strained word she and Seth spoke to each other, gritting his teeth at every smile she gave the other man—false and uncertain though they may have been. He actually snorted when Seth rewarded her acquiescence by promising her a life of unending happiness and contentment by his side.

At the rude noise, Gillian turned. "Do you doubt it, Lord Kilpatrick?" she asked him.

"Hell, no," Rhys drawled. "If your idea of happiness is wealth beyond avarice and your vision of contentment empty erotic pleasures in a marriage devoid of emotion."

She blinked. But quickly recovered. "What's wrong with being rich? And you've forgotten something even more important. As chosen consort to the most powerful immortal in the world, I will also be granted incredible powers when I become immortal myself. I could squash a man like you with a single thought."

He threw back a gulp of his wine for fortitude. "It's true. If that's the sort of thing that appeals."

Her chin inched up. "What woman wouldn't want such immense power and influence?"

Her. He barely resisted rolling his eyes at the performance. "A woman with a heart?" he muttered at the blatant lie.

Her throat convulsed. "Hearts are fickle," she said with a perfectly straight face. "I certainly hope you didn't take our meaningless affair seriously, Lord Kilpatrick." She laughed, a weak, almost choking sound. "For my heart truly belongs to another now." She tossed an all-white smile at Seth, then leveled her gaze back at Rhys. "Any *tendre* you and I may have shared was just a passing fancy. It is in the past, over and done now."

If she hadn't tried to be so damned convincing—a sure sign she'd been threatened as he had—he would have laughed out loud.

As it was, he suppressed his instinctive retort,

took another swallow of wine and did his best to appear indifferent.

"How fortuitous," he drawled, playing his assigned part loud enough for those concerned to hear, and striving not to let the sarcasm bleed through. "For I, too, have come to my senses about our little dalliance. You understand it was just a strategy to get you here to Khepesh, into the bed of our lord and leader. All in a day's work."

She winced. "Okay. Well, that's good."

He raised his goblet again and she turned resolutely away. But a few heartbeats later he felt the brush of her fingers against his trouser leg. Was she mad? After a second of shock and suddenly stone sober, he dropped his hand to his lap and wove her seeking fingers with his. Telling her with his gentle touch of the despair and longing in his breaking heart.

She was indeed a brave woman to defy Seth in this blatant manner. He yearned to lift her fingers to his lips and press a kiss to them—and warn her of the terrible danger she was putting herself in by refusing to bend to Seth-Aziz's command. He might have been tolerant of her rebellion thus far, but he'd soon put a swift and decisive stop to it.

Rhys rubbed along the length of her thumb and squeezed her fingers with his. All too soon she slipped her hand away.

But several minutes later she caught his eye while sipping her wine. "I didn't mean it," she mouthed.

He dabbed his lips with his napkin. "You think I don't know that? What did they threaten you with?"

"Your banishment." She reached for a sweet-meat. "You?"

"My severed head."

She dropped her spoon with a clatter. A trio of *shabtis* rushed to her aid and the exchange was ended when Seth glared at him suspiciously. Rhys leaned lazily back in his chair and pretended drunken indifference. But what he really felt was fury. Fury and helplessness.

One word kept echoing in his mind.

Duty. Seth saw taking Gillian as his god-damn *duty.* When Rhys longed to love and cherish her forever…

It wasn't right. Serving the god was supposed

to bring an eternity of pleasure and contentment. Up until now it had. At least he'd thought so. But he realized that somewhere along the way things had gotten twisted around. He feared Khepesh was going the way of Petru—bright in appearance but dark of spirit.

Too bad there wasn't a damn thing he could do about it.

Unbidden, Seth's earlier words returned to Rhys. *Haru-Re has tried for ages to recruit you. Why not let him?* He blinked, then slowly an idea began to form in his mind.

On second thought, maybe there was…

Chapter 16

Eat! Drink! Be merry!
For tomorrow we shall die!
  —Imhotep, Third Dynasty architect

It took Gillian two days of feigned resignation, lying through her teeth and carefully planned subterfuge to find what she was looking for. A way out.

At last! Triumphant, she gazed at the yellowed-parchment floor plan of Khepesh that she'd managed to excavate from a long-untouched shelf in the stacks of the library.

She hadn't had much time for searching because Nephtys kept her busy for hours studying the ritual she'd be performing in two days, memorizing the ancient words of magic spells she'd need for her life in Khepesh, then each evening testing her memory on what she'd learned. Worse, the library was arranged in a totally foreign system handed down since the dawn of writing, based on the hieroglyphic alphabet—which of course wasn't really an alphabet at all, but ideograms. Good grief. Who would have thought those impromptu childhood lessons by the precocious ten-year-old Josslyn, conducted in sidewalk chalk in front of their Hyde Park Chicago home, would pay off in such unexpected and lifesaving ways? Her sister would be pleased.

A pang of homesickness stabbed through Gillian, and she wondered what her sisters were doing now. Did they miss her terribly? Or had Rhys really put a spell on them so they'd never questioned her disappearance? She almost hoped he had. She didn't like to think of the sorrow she might be putting them through.

Which was exactly why she was doing this.

Of course, she'd been shouldering her own share of sorrow these last two days. Rhys had avoided her completely since the welcome feast. Which was a good thing. Really, it was. If he hadn't been making sure their paths didn't cross, she'd have been the one doing it. As much as she longed to see him, his death or banishment was too high a price to pay for continuing a relationship doomed to end in grief.

Brushing aside forlorn thoughts of those she loved, she concentrated hard and studied the parchment floor plan, looking for remnants of the traditional Old Kingdom tomb architecture that had to be hidden somewhere within the rabbit warren of Khepesh's rooms. The yellowed-parchment plan was so old, even she recognized that big bits of the current palace were missing from the drawing. No doubt, the palace had been expanded and remodeled countless times over the millennia of its existence.

She just needed to find the original tomb of Seth-Aziz. The one she'd discovered in the side of the cliff that day with Mehmet and Dawar. A day that seemed a lifetime ago.

She knew there was no possible way she

could escape through the monumental silver double doors of the Great Western Gate, which she'd come through with Rhys. But if she found the inside of the old, abandoned tomb, maybe, just maybe, she could find the hidden sliding-stone passageway and slip out through it unnoticed.

She had to try.

Her eye caught on something the drawing revealed that she hadn't expected. "Oh, wow," she exclaimed softly. "Secret passages!"

She'd had enough experience as a child traipsing after her father on his digs and surveys that she had no doubt about what she was seeing. Like the hidden sliding-block mechanism she'd discovered, secret passageways were also a rare but telling architectural feature during the Ptolemaic period. Eagerly she sought out the revealing narrow lines that marked their routes through the palace. Khepesh seemed to have its fair share, connecting the various wings in a concealed network that hinted at clandestine meetings and illicit affairs. There were even two passages that ended inside the temple compound close to her rooms. But her excitement deflated as she realized not one of the hidden passageways led to the outside world. She'd have to stick to her original plan. The old tomb with its sliding-stone entrance was her only chance.

Not to flee Khepesh. No, she had come to accept that her life as she'd once known it was over. Even if she managed to get far, far away, Seth would surely find her and bring her back. Or kill her. Of that there was no doubt whatsoever. She knew too much. The secrets of the *per netjer* were too precious to risk her talking.

She was not willing to die for their secrets—not a chance. Nor was she willing to be turned into a zombie. Her only real option was to go along with their plans and hope to change their minds about her at some point...preferably sooner than later.

Any other choice on her part would also spell the death of the man she loved. Totally unacceptable. She would suffer any pain, any sacrifice, to spare his life.

No, she must accept her fate.

But she must get a message to her sisters. To tell them she was fine, and not to worry about her. But more importantly, to let them know their mother may still be alive and that Gillian was searching for her. That she'd get word to them somehow when she had news.

All she needed was to slip out for an hour or two. Just enough time to find someone to deliver her note. Then she'd come back and face her fate as bravely as she could.

After all, there were far worse things than living a life of luxury as the wife of a vampire demigod. Forever.

Weren't there?

At the height of the afternoon heat, when the priestesses of the temple and nearly all of Khepesh were in quiet repose, Gillian set her plans in motion. The good news was that she would have no trouble locating the entrance to the old tomb. It hadn't been sealed, or even disguised. The bad news was that the only way to reach it was through a portal in the constantly-in-use council chamber.

Time was ticking away. She had to do this today. Who knew when she'd next get the chance? So from a hiding place with a good view of the chamber door, she settled down to watch for her best opportunity.

She caught a break when the council members, who were still debating day and night how to answer Haru-Re's threat, adjourned for a few hours' rest. As the last counselor left the chamber and exchanged a few words with the guardian of the door, she managed to slip past them into the darkened room, secreting herself behind a chair until the guard closed and locked the door with a loud *snick*.

She was stuck now. Committed.

Pulse thundering like a herd of hippos, she whispered a magical phrase Nephtys had taught her, to raise the level of flame on one of the ever-burning torch sconces on the wall. It sprang to life, and she lifted the torch from its holder, needing it to illuminate her hand-drawn map and light her way through the dark, disused tunnels.

Crawling through the outside opening, she had to sit just inside the mouth of the tomb for ten full minutes before her eyes adjusted to the blinding summer sunlight of the Egyptian desert. After three days and nights below ground in the realm of the God of Darkness, she felt like a groundhog emerging on February second.

She peeked out from between the towering sandstone cliffs of the *gebel,* getting her bearings. There was no trick to finding civilization—and an appropriate messenger. She just had to head for the Nile River Road, clearly visible less than a kilometer beyond the foot of the *gebel.* She made quick work of the hike down the steep path to the valley below, and was just leaning her butt against a large boulder to take a sip of water when the sound of falling pebbles alerted her. Someone was coming! Swiftly, she ducked behind the boulder.

A donkey rounded the corner carrying a welcome familiar figure. She let out a breath of relief.

"Mehmet!" she called, jumping out from her hiding place.

"Miss!" He greeted her with popping eyes. "But… Where…? How…?" His gaze darted nervously up the cliffs to the hidden tomb. "Are you dead, miss?" he asked, far too earnestly for comfort.

"No, Mehmet. I'm not dead. And I really need you to do me a favor."

"Yes, yes," he said, his hands clutching the rope tied around his donkey's muzzle, his bare heels gripping its belly as if he wanted to kick it to get the hell out of there, but didn't dare. "Anything, miss."

She walked over to him, reaching into the pocket of the simple cotton dress she'd donned for her excursion. She pulled out an envelope containing the letter she'd carefully composed, and held it up. "Mehmet, I need you to deliver this to my sisters. Can you do that?"

He eyed it uneasily, then glanced around again. "Certainly. Of course, miss."

He jerked his hand out to take the envelope, but his donkey suddenly shied, letting out a loud bray, and his grab missed. He cursed roundly in Arabic. She was glad she didn't understand most of it.

"Boys your age shouldn't know those words," admonished a deep, masculine voice from the trail above them.

Oh. Crap.

This could get ugly.

* * *

Rhys stepped out from the shelter of the *gebel* where he'd shifted from al Fahl back to his human form, fuming at what he saw. How in the name of Isis had Gillian escaped Khepesh?

"What the *hell* do you think you're doing, woman?" he ground out.

"What does it look like I'm doing?" she retorted, whipping something behind her back.

"Sentencing me to death, that's what," he shot back. He should be angry with her, but he couldn't find it beneath his fury at Seth. Hell—at himself, for getting into this situation to begin with.

She let out a gasp of denial. "No! I was coming back! I swear I was."

His brows hiked. "You really expect me to believe you managed to break free only to return to your perceived enslavement?"

"Yes!" Her bravado deflated. "Because they'd blame you. I'd never let them hurt you because of me, Rhys. I couldn't."

He regarded her for a long moment, and read the truth of it in her eyes. "Then why leave at all?"

She bit her lip. "Just something I had to do."

Ah. This was more believable. It didn't take a genius to figure out what she'd hidden behind her back. Unfortunately, he couldn't let her complete her mission.

He exhaled, grimaced, then tossed a leather pouch to Mehmet. "Here's your reward, *walad*. Now, be gone with you. Breathe a word of this to a soul and you can count on being Seth-Aziz's next sacrifice."

"Yes, sir! I mean, no, sir!" Wide-eyed, the kid slammed his heels into the donkey's sides and trotted off at full speed.

"Reward?" Gillian said indignantly over the clatter of hooves. "You *bribed* him to rat me out?"

"Better me than your future husband." Rhys approached her and held out his palm. "Okay. Hand it over."

She backed away, lifting her chin. "What?"

"Whatever you're hiding from me."

She took another step backward. "No."

What made this woman believe she could be so damn defiant? And why did her feistiness only make him want her more than he already did?

He ground his teeth, debating whether he should take her in his arms and kiss her to within an inch of her life, or put her over his knee and spank her. His cock stirred at the thought of doing either.

But here was not the place.

"Fine. Keep it. I'm going to shift now, and when I do, I want you to climb up. Do you hear me?"

"You're taking me back there?" she asked in alarm. Her breasts lifted and fell in rhythm with her quickened breaths. Distracting his gaze. And other parts of his body.

He made up his mind. "Eventually. But first we're going to my place."

Surprise lanced through her expression. "Won't that be dangerous?"

"Extremely."

"Then why?"

He pressed his mouth into a thin line. How about that he'd rather go to his death than forfeit the chance to have her under him just one more time before giving her up for good?

"Stupid, bloody question."

He closed the distance between them and pulled her into his arms, crushing his lips to hers. She let out a noise of surprise, then melted into him. She whispered his name and it sounded like a prayer to the gods. She opened to him and she tasted like sweet, black cherries and dark, forbidden love. And in that instant, he knew he would do anything to have her. To keep her.

Before he lost complete control, he whirled in a circle, chanting the powerful words that would turn him into al Fahl.

She clung to him, burying her face in his hair, and swung onto the back of the stallion he'd become. Putting her life into his hands in more ways than one. He reared up, then started to gallop, devouring the miles of desolate sand to reach the secret *wadi* where his house lay hidden. He didn't miss a beat when he shifted back, sweeping her into his arms and striding through the stables and the kitchen, past the startled servants, and straight to his bedroom.

They tore at each other's clothes, stripping

one another naked as their mouths refused to relinquish the wet fusion of their kisses.

"You're mine," he said over and over as they kissed and touched, and renewed their unspoken vows. "Mine. *Mine*."

"Yes. Oh, yes," she moaned as he threw her onto the bed and mounted her in a single forceful movement. His cock scythed in, seeking the tight, wet heat of her. He grunted, holding back the explosive need to take her hard and fast. He wanted her to remember something better than mindless coupling for what might be their last time, if later things went badly.

"Oh, Rhys," she said breathlessly. "I was sure you didn't want me anymore."

"How can you say that?" he groaned, pulling back to look into her eyes.

"I haven't seen you for two days. I thought you'd accepted Seth's orders and given me up...."

"Darling, I'll always want you, and will never give up hope of having you for my own. I need you to know that absolutely, no matter what you hear about me, no matter what happens."

She wrapped her arms tightly around him.

"You're scaring me. You make it sound so dire. So final."

"Promise you'll trust me, Gillian. Just promise me that."

"I do. I promise," she whispered, concern etching her face. "What are you planning?"

He smiled. "Right now, to make love to my woman," he murmured, and started to thrust.

He made it last, and he made it good. He used every trick he knew, physical and magical, to increase his own potency and her pleasure. He knew he was up against a formidable rival in Seth. Vampires possessed sexual powers unheard of in any other beings, and could gift her with more pleasure than Rhys ever hoped to. But he had one advantage that Seth didn't.

He had her love. And she his.

And in the end that counted far more than all the erotic pleasures in the world.

"They're going to know, aren't they?"

Gillian's insides fought a queasy battle between contentment and panic.

It was hard not to feel amazingly good wrapped in Rhys's arms, her body throbbing from the best sex she'd ever had in her life, her heart bursting with the knowledge that he truly loved her. He must, to take this kind of risk to be with her. But she couldn't shake the insidious dread sneaking through her veins that Nephtys was even now watching them in the waters of her damned scrying bowl, Seth by her side, shouting orders to Sheikh Shahin to sharpen his sword for a beheading.

Gillian didn't know what she would do if any harm came to Rhys. She'd rather live through a loveless eternity than see him suffer because of her imprudent actions.

Not that it was wrong to try and contact her sisters to let them know she was okay. Quite the opposite. But she should have waited. It would have been far better to sneak out and deliver her letter after all this drama with Seth had settled down.

"They'll know we made love, won't they?" she repeated when Rhys didn't answer. She glanced up at him.

He was on his side, head resting on his palm over his bent elbow, gazing at her with an inscrutable look on his handsome face.

And, lord, was he ever handsome. Smooth, angular features boasted long-lashed, slumberous eyes and sculpted lips. His shoulders were impossibly broad, his arms corded with strength, his chest muscular and ripped, his waist narrow and his horseman's thighs hard as iron. Not to mention his long, thick stallion's cock, ever at the ready to rise from its rest amid thick black curls.

Just looking at the man's nude body made her weak with desire, ready to spread her legs and beg him to take her just one more time.

"Maybe," he finally answered, making her scramble to remember what the question was. "Do you care if Seth knows we defied him?"

She closed her eyes and stretched out on the bed. "Not at the moment. Ask me again when he's about to drain all the blood from my body."

Rhys frowned. "Not remotely funny."

"Sorry." She turned and nestled up against him. "It's either that or cry. Up until now I've been trying my damnedest not to think about the future, but… What's going to happen to us, Rhys? Seriously."

"I honestly don't know. Seth could be merciful. We've been friends for a long time. And his interest in you seems more tied to Nephtys's vision than any real attraction."

She sighed. "*Duty.* That's what he called me." She didn't want Seth's romantic interest, but still. That stung a little.

"Don't take it personally. He's always been distant with women. Not much luck with females over the years."

"Which is why he sends *you* out to do his bidding." She poked his ribs none too gently. "Mr. Charming Seducer."

"Hey!" He rolled her under him and wedged his hips between her thighs. "I think you will not have to worry about that any longer," he said drily. "Even if I survive Seth's displeasure, my days as master steward have no doubt run their course."

She gazed up at him, feeling love and guilt and distress all rolled into one giant lump in her throat. "I'm sorry, Rhys. I'm so sorry I've come between you and your friend. God! I wish I could go back to before all this started. Back to that day I was searching the *gebel* for your grave site with Mehmet. He *told* me not to go into that damn tomb, but would I listen?" She squeezed her eyes shut.

"Do you wish you had?" he asked softly. "Do you wish you'd taken his advice and never gone into that tomb? Never found the secret of Khepesh? Never met me?"

She searched her heart. *Did she?*

Oh, God, if she had the chance to do it all over again, would she choose to pass by that fateful tomb, and never be parted from her sisters? Never have to face an eternity as consort to a vampire? Never meet the man she would love until the end of time?

She swallowed and felt the warmth of tears trickling down her cheeks. "No," she whispered, knowing that having these few precious moments with him made all her future anguish worthwhile. "I would do everything exactly the same, every last minute."

Chapter 17

I love you through the daytimes,
In the dark,
Through all the long divisions of the
night…

—*Song on an Eastern Vessel*

Sunset was approaching as they left Rhys's house, walking hand in hand to the meadow behind the stables. The air had cooled from the scorching heat of day to a pleasant evening warmth, and a soft breeze played with Gillian's pale hair, messing it up even more than his fingers had earlier. She looked fragile, but oh, so beautiful.

"I dread going back," she said.

So did he. "Then let's stay out for a while longer."

The sky was a kaleidoscope of dazzling color. Oranges and pinks swirled in the west around the dying orb of the sun, topped by a meringue of blues and purples that melded into the indigo of the night sky to the east.

It was the kind of sunset that begged to be enjoyed and revered, offered up to the gods as a token of earthly devotion.

He shifted into al Fahl and she climbed on his back, and together they rode out into the vast desert, up to the highest point on the *gebel*.

There they stood, the lone woman and the wild beast she'd so thoroughly tamed, watching the ark of the sun be devoured by the mouth of the Night God. She stroked his equine neck with loving hands, like she had stroked his body as they'd made love earlier. He could feel her strong knees pressed into his ribs, her silky, bare thighs wrapped around him, the pushed-up hem of her dress an insubstantial flutter against his thick hide. The sultry heat from between her parted legs insinuated itself into his consciousness, bringing him to full erection. He could smell the scent of her, of him, of their intense and fevered sex, clinging to her skin, his own essence still deep within her, proclaiming her to all as his.

As the last burning vestige of the sun was eclipsed by the black rim of the Western Desert, he raised his head and let out a powerful whinny, joining the chorus of jackals and wildcats and the other night creatures that greeted the darkness. All around the desert, the voices of the night lifted, a cacophonous noise to celebrate the daily defeat of the sun god Re-Horakhti to the sovereignty of Set-Sutekh, Lord of the Moon.

Rhys felt Gillian shiver in fear at the unearthly sound and lean forward to cling to al Fahl's mane. She didn't know that no creature would dare harm her because she belonged to the *per netjer* of the Guardian of Darkness and rode the ghost stallion.

He reared up, turning, and started the chant,

catching her in his arms when she tumbled from her seat as he shifted back to human form.

He kissed her deep and hard, and shoved her dress from her shoulders, peeling it down her body until she was naked before him. His arousal still throbbed for her, thick as a stallion's and with a stallion's appetite.

He splayed the buttons of his trousers, letting his desire spring free, then urged her to her knees in the sand. She looked up at him, her eyes reflecting the glitter of the stars and moon above. Slowly, she moved closer, her lips parting and her tongue reaching for his rampant cock as their gazes met and locked.

She painted his turgid flesh with hot, wet strokes while she wrapped her fingers around him and squeezed. He grunted, a harsh, animal sound that vibrated from deep in his lungs. Her lips opened wider and enveloped him, almost bringing him to his own knees.

His voracious hunger exploded as she worked him. He shot his fingers through her hair and wound its length around his fist as though she were the horse and he the rider. When he couldn't stand it a moment longer, he dragged her mouth off him, and dropped down in front of her. He took her lips, and tasted himself on her. Desire flamed through his body, his carnal flesh still feeling the echoes of his recent shift.

Fist still in her hair, he quickly turned her, pushed her to her hands and knees, and with a mighty thrust, mounted her from behind.

She cried out his name and arched her back, meeting his thrust with one of her own. Accepting his domination. Urging him to go faster, harder.

The animal in him thrilled to his possession of her. As did the man. They rode their passion to the brink of ecstasy, faster, harder, deeper than ever before, then together they closed their eyes and left the world behind in a blinding explosion of hearts and bodies.

In the dark desert night, with the stars and planets as witnesses, Rhys knew she had become his one true mate.

"Why did you do it?"

Rhys wasn't sure to what Gillian was referring. *It* could be any number of things. "Do what?" he asked.

"Join the *per netjer* of Set-Sutekh."

"Ah."

They were wrapped in his Bedouin cloak, lying in each other's arms on the warm sand and gazing up at the vast blanket of stars that twinkled overhead in an obsidian sky. Neither was in any hurry to face what awaited them at Khepesh, so they pretended it didn't exist. For now.

"I mean, you were a British lord, a man of considerable wealth and privilege, with a life anyone would envy. What made you give it all up, for…for this?"

He pushed out a breath, casting over the memories he carried of his birthplace. The cold images and feelings had softened with time, but none were particularly content or happy, even seen through the tempering lens of a century and a quarter.

"I don't see it so much as giving up anything, but as gaining something else. Something much better."

"What?" she asked. "What did you find here that you didn't have before?"

"A home. Family. People who understand me and need me."

She canted over his chest and rested her chin on her hands. "But your real family seems nice. The ones alive today, anyway. They care about what became of you."

He made a face. "They care about the Kilpatrick name," he corrected. "Heaven forbid my legacy besmirch it. Which reminds me, you should send a report to them saying you didn't find my grave. The last thing we need is some nosy Kilpatrick showing up looking for it, or you."

She nodded. "I will. But I still don't understand what made you choose Khepesh as your home. You could have just run off to America or Australia and lived like a king. Why join a cult in an uncivilized country, serving a god you don't believe in?"

"Egypt is hardly uncivilized. It's the very cradle of human civilization," he reminded her.

"Don't tell that to the Mesopotamians," she drawled.

He chuckled and pressed a kiss onto her forehead. "And I never said I don't believe in Set-Sutekh. To me, he's just one aspect of the all-encompassing God of creation. His personi-fication might appear primitive to us, but the meaning he carries is just as relevant today as it was when mankind first emerged from the caves."

"A message of darkness?"

"Darkness is the natural state of the universe. Just look above us. All dark, except for an in-significant scattering of burning cosmic dust. Darkness is the glue that binds it all together. To hold it in awe is to pay homage to the mys-tery of creation."

She digested that for a moment. "But... doesn't it follow then that Re-Horakhti, the God of Light and Sun, represents knowledge and the rise of consciousness?" she persisted. "Why not choose the god of reason and enlightenment?"

"You've *met* Haru-Re, right?" he asked drily.

She half smiled. "He's just the priest, not the god."

Rhys sighed. "I suppose." He thought for a moment. "I guess I was drawn to the dark-ness because of my dissolute lifestyle. Back then, I was a rake and a hellion, and thrived in the nightlife that supported my less-than-gentlemanly tendencies. But I've come to realize that darkness itself has nothing to do with wickedness. Wickedness resides solely in the man who exploits it."

She quietly digested that, too, then asked, "Then why the two gods? What is the true difference between darkness and light?"

"There is none," he said. "It's what men make of them that counts. It doesn't matter which aspect we serve. In the end, mankind needs both the darkness and the light to survive."

They watched the unfolding of the sky for several long minutes, content in their closeness, two matched souls in the vast solitude of the desert night.

"So…" she said at length, drawing her finger lightly down his body. "How wicked were you, exactly? Back in the day?"

He smiled, his body stirring at her touch. "Very wicked."

"What kind of sinful things did you do?" she asked.

"Oh, all sorts of very naughty things."

"Tell me," she whispered. "Tell me everything."

"Hmm," he murmured, rolling her under him. "I'd much rather show you."

"She's gone, my lady. I can't find Miss Haliday anywhere."

Nephtys took the *shemat*'s news calmly. She hadn't needed the Eye of Horus to predict *this* development. The girl was headstrong and willful. And head over heels in love. "And Lord Kilpatrick?"

The *shemat* shuffled her feet. "Gone, as well. But he frequently visits his home aboveground. His absence may be unconnected."

Nephtys sent the acolyte a withering glance. "Perhaps." But not terribly likely. "Thank you. I'll take care of it." She waved a hand in dismissal.

She was sitting at her vanity, touching up her makeup after a much-needed nap. She hadn't been sleeping well. She pushed out a sigh and met her own eyes in the mirror. Today she felt truly as old as her years on earth.

What would she do about these two? They seemed determined to bring down the worst punishment upon themselves. All because of love.

She made a face. *Love*. The most treacherous of all emotions! Like a spider it lured one into its web with sweet temptations, then poisoned one with its sting, devoured one's body, finally to discard the empty shell of one's heart without a second thought, moving on to its next hapless victim.

She'd be doing the lovers a favor if she urged her brother simply to put them out of their wretched misery.

Unbidden, thoughts of the man who still held her heart captive whispered through her body, raising goose bumps of long-banked passion. What would it feel like to have a man love her so much he was willing to risk all for a moment in her arms? To face death for a brush of her lips?

She shivered with longing. Bringing to mind the taste of her lover's kiss, the weight of his body, the thrust of his hard flesh as he took her.

She let her head fall back as it had when he'd held her and kissed her and told her he'd never let her go. Her hand moved from the vanity to her knee, then trailed upward, seeking the moist warmth between her thighs. She touched herself, letting a soft sound of frustrated need slip past her lips.

"Haru-Re," she whispered. *My love.*

And suddenly, he was there with her, her strong, princely lover, and she was under him, clinging to the golden spindles of his bed as he sipped blood from her neck and slowly slayed her body with his awesome powers, robbing her of every thought but of pleasing him.

"I have missed you, my only heart," he murmured in her ear as his fangs grazed her lips, leaving thin trails of her own blood behind. Shivers of pleasure spilled over her, hot and intense. "Come back to me," he whispered. "I need you. I want you here by my side."

His cock plunged deep into her, filling her, possessing her, until she screamed in exquisite pleasure. *Yes, oh, yes!*

His hands found her breasts, his mouth following close behind. He tongued her nipples, then sucked deeply, one then the other, then back again. With each draw, she felt the prick of his fangs in her soft flesh, and with every pierce a climax swept through her, each more powerful than the last. His tongue lapped at the beads of blood and it was like aftershocks of the earthquake that was his sensual power.

"Come back," he whispered. "Come to Petru and I promise you pleasures such as you have never felt, power such as you have never possessed. *Come back to me.*"

"Yes," she moaned. "Yes, my love."

His cock expanded within her like a ghostly, ethereal presence, taking over her body, filling every inch of her flesh and blood with its chimerical manifestation. She released her will to him, as she had always done, and he took her over completely, making love to every cell of her being, rocking her universe, sending her to another plane of pleasure. It felt as though their very souls were joined as one. And when she came for him, it was like the sun breaking at dawn, filling her body with the electric life force of the cosmos, coming alive and transcending into pure, unending pleasure.

She didn't know when she'd lost consciousness, nor when she'd returned to herself and started to stir. Her breath still came fast and furious, her pulse pounding through her as if the armies of the pharaoh were chasing her.

"Sweet Isis," she murmured, squeezing her eyes even tighter in consternation. What had happened to her? This had not been a simple fantasy of self-pleasure.

A vision?

She had never before experienced one of such intensity. Or so disturbing. What could it mean?

But no. If it was a vision, it had to have been a false prophecy. She would *never* give her betrayer a promise like that. A promise to a demigod was binding, on pain of death. And she would never go back to Haru-Re! *Never.*

Just a dream. She was exhausted. She must have fallen asleep and had a nightmare.

She took a deep, cleansing breath. Yes. That's all it was, thank the merciful goddess! A vivid, upsetting nightmare. And no one could be held to things they did or promises they made in the upside-down twilight world of sleep.

She opened her eyes in relief.

And instantly froze in horror.

"No!" she cried in anguished disbelief.

For there, glistening on her lips in stark accusation, lay twin tracks of blood trailing a path down her throat to two round, ragged punctures.

Chapter 18

Double doors swung open,
The half-seen inner chambers—
Out she'll be soon,
Furious I followed.

—Papyrus Harris 500

With his new certainty of their love so vividly imprinted on his mind and body, Rhys found the strength he needed to do what he knew he must. It wouldn't be easy, and he was just as likely to end up headless as with the prize he sought, but the knowledge that Gillian felt as deeply for him as he did for her made the danger worth facing.

But she wasn't going to like this part.

He didn't bother taking her back in through the old tomb, but arrived at the Great Western Gate with his hand wrapped firmly around her wrist and the letter to her sisters tucked carefully into the folds of his robes.

"What are you doing?" she protested, no doubt wondering at the abrupt change in him.

"Just trust me."

"But Rhys—"

"Follow my lead and we may have a chance."

"Don't I get any say in this?"

He tried not to hear the hurt in her voice and reminded himself he was doing it for her. "Not this time."

The doors swung open and he strode through them, towing her along behind, acting as though he hadn't spent the last several hours in treasonous activity that should rightly earn him the edge of a blade on his neck.

By the time they reached the audience chamber, Seth was there to greet them. Or perhaps he'd been waiting for them all along.

Well. *Greet* might be too strong a word. The high priest stood in the center of the room with a furious expression, radiating waves of red-hot anger. Nephtys stood, strangely pale, a few paces behind him, and Shahin lounged with deceptive calm against a pillar on the side, looking swarthy and confident as ever, his blade at his side.

The least hesitation and Rhys knew he'd be done for.

"You should have a care with your possessions, my lord!" he said boldly to Seth, forcing Gillian to her knees before him with a spell and a quick touch on her shoulder. "It seems some of them are of a mind to stray."

His audacity bought him a brief reprieve. Seth's eyes narrowed on Gillian for an instant, then lifted to bore through Rhys's. His mouth thinned.

"Strayed straight into your bed, I perceive," he barked, wrinkling his nose in disgust. "Her skin carries the smell of you, Englishman. You could at least make an attempt to conceal your treason."

"It would be of no use, my lord," he answered

unflinchingly. "She will always smell of me. You can kill me and take her for the next thousand years, and she will still smell of me. For she is mine now, and mine alone."

Gillian let out a gasp. "I'm not!" she cried. "I swear I'm not! I know I'm to be yours, Seth-Aziz. I just… It was *my* fault. We'd been together before and I…I was bespelled by him. I wanted him again. He didn't want to touch me, but I seduced him. I—"

Rhys's rapid heartbeat skipped in anxiety at her brave defense of him. But before he could open his mouth to deny it, Seth slashed a hand up.

"Enough!" Seth jetted out a virulent oath. "Your lies are transparent, woman! Do you take me for a complete fool?"

Nephtys moved forward and put a calming hand on his arm. *"Hadu,"* she said. "Remember, a woman's actions are ruled by her heart, not her reason. You must show Gillian mercy in her blindness."

Seth shook her off, stalked a few paces, then spun back on a toe. Again he scorched them with a look, taking several angry breaths. "Your loyalty is commendable, Miss Haliday. I only hope one day you'll feel such devoted allegiance to your lord and master."

She swallowed heavily. "I—I'm sure I w-will," she stammered unconvincingly.

Rhys eased a layer of tension from his shoulders. They might yet live through the day.

Seth's jaw clenched. He motioned jerkily to Shahin and Nephtys. "Get them out of here before I truly lose my temper. You are both confined to your quarters until I decide what to do with you."

"As you command, my lord." Rhys inclined his head. "But before you judge the woman, there's something you should see." He produced her envelope from his robes. "She was not trying to flee Khepesh. She was only trying to deliver this."

Gillian cried out and leaped up from her knees, feeling her pocket and trying to grab it from him all at the same time. "No! How did you get that? You have no right to take it!"

Seth's hand made a slight wave and Gillian halted in her tracks. Her eyes widened. Rhys handed him the envelope. He was sorry to hurt her, but one day she would understand why he had to do it. He could see that Seth was also taken aback by his unexpected actions. It wounded him that his friend was surprised. Although he'd given Seth ample reason to doubt him concerning Gillian, he would never compromise the safety of Khepesh.

Wordlessly, Seth slid open the envelope, extracted the paper inside and read it.

The high priest frowned, cleared his throat and glanced at Gillian. With a quick gesture, he reversed the spell and let her move. She sucked in a breath, opened her mouth to protest, but wisely kept her peace when Seth glowered at her.

"Have you read this?" he asked Rhys.

"No. I assume it's addressed to her sisters."

"It is." He passed the missive.

Rhys read the neatly inked letter.

My Dear Loving Sisters,
I hope this note finds you well and happy.
OMG! I'm in love! He is a wonderful man
who has already given me the stars and

the moon. There is talk of a wedding soon.
Be thrilled for me!

Incredible news—our beloved mother
may still be alive. I am following every
clue to find out the truth about her disap-
pearance. Speaking of which, don't worry,
I have not disappeared. Am spending time
with my new man and playing detective. I
promise to be in touch soon.
Love and hugs, Jelly Bean

Rhys had prayed with all his heart Gillian
had not been foolish enough to tell her sisters
anything about Khepesh or the things she'd seen
there, and was gratified—and very relieved—to
see his faith in her had been upheld.

"Fairly convincing proof that Gillian intended to return to Khepesh," he stated, sending
her a smile as he returned the letter to Seth. She
refused to meet his gaze.

"What is this about your mother?" Seth
asked her sharply.

She hesitated long enough that Rhys supplied the relevant information, and explained
about the photo and the proof they'd discovered

in the library that Isobelle Haliday had been taken to Petru. "I promised I'd help her discover her mother's fate since her abduction by our enemy."

Shahin suddenly looked like he wanted to kill something, but Seth's gaze softened a fraction. Behind him, Nephtys swayed, looking stricken at the mention of her former captor. Maybe she could be persuaded to seek a vision on the matter, after all.

"If your mother is in the clutches of Haru-Re," Seth said, "I'm afraid nothing good has befallen her. I'm very sorry."

Gillian pressed her lips together and didn't comment. Knowing her, she'd believe her mother's ruination only when she saw evidence with her own eyes.

"As for your wedding," Seth went on, "I am glad you are thrilled. I have decided you may have until the transformation ceremony to prepare yourself. We shall be joined on the day after."

Two days!

Gillian blanched, her lips parting in dismay. Rhys's blood rushed into his hands as he balled them into tight fists to keep from reaching for a weapon.

He was outmatched in this battle and he knew it. He'd win the war with Seth over Gillian, not with strength, but with cunning. How could he hope to have a feasible plan in place in two days' time?

"If I'm no longer needed, I have work to do," he managed to grind out.

To his surprise, Seth carefully refolded Gillian's letter, inserted it back in the envelope and handed it to Shahin. "When next you're aboveground, see it's delivered," he ordered, then looked at Rhys.

Still furious, his friend had nevertheless regained control of his emotions. His back straight and tall, he was once more the unflappable figure of supreme authority. "Khepesh will always need you, Lord Kilpatrick," he said. "I've been more than patient with your grave misbehavior, but I have reached my limit. Do *not* make me do something we would all bitterly regret. Miss Haliday shall be my consort, and if I have to take her right here and now in front of you to convince you of my seriousness, by the gods,

I will!" To illustrate his point, he took a stride toward Gillian and grabbed her by the hair.

She cried out, her face ashen.

Rhys choked down a roar of protest. "That won't be necessary. We are both your obedient servants."

"Good. Now, say goodbye." Seth set his jaw in rigid determination. "For all contact between you is to cease immediately." He didn't need to add *or suffer the consequences*. The threat was there in his burning gaze. He turned to Gillian. "And you, Miss Haliday. I expect your full and willing participation in the ceremony in two days, and for our joining the day after that. Do I make myself clear?"

"Yes," she said, her voice cracking.

"Good. Now leave me," Seth growled, "all of you!" and stalked from the room.

Late that night, Gillian was still shaking from the audience with Seth-Aziz. She wrapped her arms around her middle as she closed her chamber door under the watchful eyes of Nephtys.

"We don't allow weapons in the temple," the priestess warned, "but there's a guard posted at the portal. Do not even think about trying to escape again."

"Don't worry. I don't have a death wish," she muttered, and shut the door in the woman's face.

Rude? Maybe. But she was pretty pissed off about being treated like a pawn in a game that didn't concern her. Hello? *She* was the one who had to be married to a freaking vampire for the rest of eternity!

It wasn't even having sex with him that bothered her so much—okay, fine, yeah, it did, a lot—but just as bad was being completely invisible, her wishes and opinions dismissed as totally irrelevant.

Which she realized was the plight women had suffered throughout much of history, and to which many women around the world were still being subjected.

She didn't like it.

She did not like it one damn bit.

But what could she do? The choice was either submit or Rhys would die. Possibly herself, too.

To Gillian, life was a precious gift. She'd

never been able to forgive her father for giving up and walking into the desert to end it all. He'd claimed he loved her mother too much to go on without her...but if he were alive now, he would be with her again soon, if Gillian succeeded in rescuing her.

Where there was life, there was always hope.

She truly believed that.

Which was why, even if she had to live through many unhappy years to come, she would never, ever, give up hope of being with Rhys again.

Somehow she had to tell him that. Beg him not to do anything stupid, in anger or desperation, and end up dead. She couldn't face the prospect of a forever without him.

Of course, wandering the halls of Khepesh for all to see in order to reach him and tell him that would get them both killed even faster.

And then she remembered. The secret passageways she'd discovered on the floor plan from the library! There were two that started here in the temple compound—one in Seth's private dressing room, and one in the inner sanctum behind the central altar. But where did they end up? She closed her eyes and tried to picture the floor plan. She was pretty sure one of them ended in the residential wing where Rhys had his rooms.

Did she dare?

Her heart thumped painfully in her chest. She had to risk it. She was terrified Rhys might try to stop the ceremony otherwise. Sacrifice his life for her. She had to tell him not to do it.

She waited until well after the torches had been lowered, the priestesses had retired to their chambers and the *haram* had grown quiet. Then she crept out and along the darkened hallways into the temple proper. It, too, lay still and silent, the diamond stars in the lapis lazuli ceiling winking at her as she felt with her fingertips along the wall of the inner sanctum for the hidden mechanism that would spring open the cleverly concealed doorway to the secret passage. Even knowing approximately where it should be—directly behind the giant obsidian sarcophagus—it took her several minutes to find it with the tip of an offering knife.

"Yes!" she murmured under her breath as

a section of the wall whispered open to reveal a claustrophobically short, narrow space behind it. People must have been a lot smaller in Ptolemaic times.

Praying fervently there were no snakes or spiders living within its tight confines, Gillian lifted her borrowed torch and ducked into the passage. And prayed even harder that she wouldn't find an armed guard at the other end.

Chapter 19

If ever, my dear one, I should not be here,
where would you offer your heart?
     —Song Cycle 1, Papyrus Harris 500

A soft knock on the door to his palace suite roused Rhys from the occupation he'd been engaged in for the past several hours: staring into space. Plotting. Planning. Seething.

"Go away!" he barked. He was in no mood for company, friend or foe.

A few seconds later there was another knock, even softer.

"By Sekhmet's breath! Leave me the hell alone!" he bellowed. "Whatever you're offering, I've no desire for it."

This time the pest hesitated nearly a full minute before knocking again. He could barely hear it, but there it came, mouse-quiet but jackal-determined.

Mithra's balls! Could a man not be left in peace to stew? He lunged up and flung open the door, about to shout down the unwelcome nuisance, but the oaths froze in his throat.

"*Je*sus!" he hissed, grasped Gillian's arm and hauled her inside, slamming her up against the wall next to the door. *"Have you lost your mind completely?"* Then he grabbed her and dragged her into his arms, wrapping her in a fierce embrace. He was shaking. Actually *shaking.* "How in blazes did you get here without being stopped?"

She burst out with something about forgotten maps and secret passages, but his mind wouldn't focus on her explanation, only on the welcome feel of her in his arms.

"Oh, Rhys, I had to see you," she said, her

voice muffled against his chest. "Just one last time before—"

"Don't!" he cut her off. He didn't want to hear it. Not from her lips. "It's not going to happen. I won't let it."

She drew back and looked up, her eyes bright with tears. "But you must! If you try to stop the ceremony, you'll be executed. It was a pure miracle Seth didn't kill you this afternoon, after goading him like that."

"He should have," Rhys ground out. "It would have been a mercy."

"No!" she cried. "I won't make it through this without you, Rhys. Even if we can't be together right now, I need to know you're close by, alive and well, dreaming of the day we can be. As will I."

He let a few moments of silence pass. "I'll always be waiting for that day, my love, but… what if I'm not close by?"

Her anxiety turned to dismay. "What do you mean?"

"I can't stay here and watch another man possess you, Gillian. I don't have it in me. I should leave Khepesh. For both our sakes."

She looked stricken. "But you can't! Wouldn't that mean giving up your immortality?"

"Not necessarily." He brushed his hand along the side of her cheek. "This isn't the only place immortals dwell."

Her eyes widened. "Rhys! You can't mean to go to Petru!"

"Seth has made it clear my position here is finished. Haru-Re wants me as a lieutenant. I'm inclined to accept his offer."

"But that's—"

"Treason?" He shook his head. "Technically, perhaps. But I could protect Khepesh. Mediate our differences. Try to counsel peace instead of the war Haru-Re seems so determined to wage."

She swallowed. "I suppose."

"And your mother. If she's there I can find her, protect her for you," he reminded her. "I would do my best to reunite you somehow."

Her expression broke into a chaos of hope and reluctance. "That would be…God, such a relief to know you were taking care of her. But, oh, Rhys, what would I do without you here, taking care of *me,* if only from a distance?"

She looked so forlorn he hugged her close. "You'd live a hell of a lot longer, if this visit is any indication of our ability to stay away from each other." He tipped up her chin. "Though I'll admit I am very, very glad you find it so hard to resist me."

A tear seeped onto her lower eyelashes. "When would you leave?"

He kissed away the tear, then kissed her forehead. "Right away. Tonight. It's best I am far away before that damned ceremony starts. If he touches you, tries to force himself on you, I won't be responsible for my actions."

She gave a barely discernible nod. "So this is it, then? The last time I'll ever see you?" More tears trickled down her cheeks.

"It won't be forever, love. I'll find a way for us to be together. I swear I'll come back for you, even if I have to battle my way through Hell to do it."

"I believe you," she whispered, then kissed him softly. "I love you, Rhys. I love you so much."

She'd never said the words before. It was so bittersweet to hear them now, when he might never hear them again. "I love you, too, Gillian, my love. Keep me always in your heart. And when you really need me, whisper my name. I'll be there to keep you safe."

They made love.

Sweet, aching, wistful love.

No tricks. No magic. Just two people whose hearts were breaking. A tender goodbye Gillian would remember as long as she lived, whether it was five days or five thousand years.

And when they lay spent in each other's arms, their last kiss lingering like nectar on their lips, reality reared up its unwelcome head and they started to fear they'd be discovered. She'd stayed too long already.

Rhys insisted on going with her through the passage to make sure she got back to her rooms at the temple without incident. The whole time her heart felt like it was shattering in a trillion pieces, leaving a dusting of sorrow along the way. And then they were there, emerging cautiously behind the row of altars, all laden with fruits to the god. There were buntings of flowers bearing dozens of flickering candles, too, as the priestesses had begun preparing the room for the ceremony.

"Don't think about it," Rhys told her. "I hate Seth with a passion right now, but…he's always treated his sacrifices with consideration."

She knew he was only trying to make her feel better, but she refused to be comforted. "I don't doubt that. But… Oh, God, Rhys! Let's run away!" She grabbed his hand and tugged him toward the exit portal. "Now. Let's just go! What happens to us, happens."

"No," he said, standing his ground and cupping her face between his palms. He peered at her earnestly. "It would be suicide. You *must* go through with the ceremony."

"But—"

"Just think of me, and I'll be there with you."

He wrapped his arms around her and gave her one last, agonized kiss.

And then he was gone.

The section of wall blocking the passage slid back into place with a quiet finality.

And once again, she was all alone.

Chapter 20

Let me drink in the shape of my love,
tall in the shuddering night!
>   —Great Heart's Ease,
>   Papyrus Chester Beaty I

The night of the ceremony had arrived, and Gillian was not too proud to admit she was terrified out of her wits.

She was about to have her blood sucked by a vampire in front of hundreds of witnesses. True, only she and Seth would be in the inner sanctum when it happened. But the sacred obsidian altar where it would take place lay directly in line with the portal to the Courtyard of the Sacred Pool, which in turn was wide-open to the huge hypostyle festival hall, and both court-yards would be filled to capacity with every one of the immortals of Khepesh.

This was it. No way out.

She groaned. Talk about insane! A few short days ago she would never have believed that any of this existed, let alone that she would be up to her eyeballs in otherworldly political intrigue!

Nephtys glanced at her, frowned, then poured a goblet of wine and handed it to her. "Drink this. It will calm your nerves."

"Can't you put some kind of spell on me?" she pleaded. "Make me unconscious so I can wake up afterward and not remember a thing?"

The priestess's brow rose. "Oh, you'll want to remember. Being bitten by a vampire is...an amazing experience. Better than any sex you've ever had."

A dull pain pressed against Gillian's chest. "Not if I don't love him."

"Trust me—" Nephtys turned abruptly to

peer at herself in the mirror, adjusting the high silver collar clasped around her neck "—love has nothing to do with it."

Gillian tipped her goblet and drank down the wine. Every last drop. Her head spun a little as the alcohol hit her bloodstream. She held out the silver cup for more. Maybe vampire fangs were like certain other male appendages, and if she drank enough wine her blood-alcohol would get Seth too drunk to perform.

She giggled at the thought. Gemma would have a field day with *that* one.

Thinking about Gemma, Gillian wondered wistfully how her sisters were doing. They must have received her note by now, if Sheikh Shahin had delivered it as Seth had ordered. Had they been surprised to hear from her? Were they worried about her?

How would they react if they knew the truth about where she was and what she was about to go through? What if they had been here now?

Despite herself, she smiled. Gemma would no doubt be taking notes like mad, fascinated by everything and everyone. Josslyn would probably be raising holy hell, giving Seth what for about abusing innocent women, storming into the sanctuary in the nick of time to save her from being drained. Probably ending up as the sacrifice herself because it would be the only way Seth could get her to shut up.

She laughed softly. God, she missed them so much!

She realized Nephtys was staring at her with puzzled amusement.

"My sisters," she explained wryly. "I was just thinking about them."

"Ah. I understand," the other woman said, gesturing for her to come over to the mirror so she could check her outfit one final time. "I'm that way with Seth. Our youthful antics can pop into my head at the most inappropriate times."

Antics? *Seth?*

"It'll be nice to have a sister," Nephtys went on, gazing kindly at her reflection. "To make new memories with."

Gillian realized with a start that she meant *her.* "Um, yeah," she quickly agreed. Then turned away to put down her goblet. Somehow she couldn't imagine them in a powwow on the floor, painting their toenails and laughing together over a bad date.

Nephtys smoothed her fingers along the elaborately embroidered stole Gillian wore over her tight, black strapless gown, touching the pattern of tiny stars that spangled the shoulders of the wrap. "I know this is difficult for you," she said. "But you are a lucky woman. The envy of every other in Khepesh. Open yourself to the pleasures of your sacrifice, Gillian. You might find you enjoy it more than you think."

"I'll try," she said, though she knew she wouldn't. She had no defense against the power and magic the vampire demigod had over her body, but she would not betray Rhys in her mind.

She gazed at her own reflection in the mirror, and was glad she barely recognized herself. Her eyes were heavily made-up, dark and sultry with kohl and black liner in the style of the ancients. Her lips were painted bloodred, her complexion pale as snow against them. Her hair had been piled in a froth of curls on her head… presumably to keep it off her neck.

Oh, God.

She reached for the goblet again, then pulled back her hand. Lord. One more sip of wine and she'd probably keel over.

Not necessarily a bad thing.

But just delaying the inevitable.

Because no matter how much she rebelled against the idea, this was really happening.

To her.

Tonight.

Oh, God.

Where was Rhys when she needed him?

As at the welcome feast, Gillian was accompanied by Nephtys and the two *shemat*s as she was walked with slow, measured steps to the middle of the hypostyle festival hall. There she was greeted by the immortals of Khepesh with raucous cheers and showers of scarlet flower petals shaped like droplets of blood. The men were bare-chested, wearing only black Bedouin trousers, with chilling black masks painted around their eyes. The women all wore sleeveless, pleated gowns of silver that turned nearly transparent when the torchlight hit them just right, and elaborate jewelry of the finest gems.

Like hers, their eyes were also made-up with black liner and kohl, each woman more beautiful than Cleopatra herself.

Gillian wasn't the only one who'd had a bit too much to drink. The mood for the ceremony was pure bacchanalia, men and women crushed together in an ebb and flow of naked limbs and breathless anticipation. The air was thickly fragrant and electric with immortal power. It sparked over her skin like sensual fur, seeking out the most secret places of her body and bringing them to life. It was impossible not to feel the excitement and eroticism of the night stroking her flesh.

Music, strange and melodic, drifted through the room, and as one, the crowd began to move back and forth in a rhythmic dance. The sensual power increased.

She gasped as it washed over her, raising goose flesh along her arms in a tingle of yearning desire, pooling between her thighs.

The wake of the crowd pulled her along toward the Courtyard of the Sacred Pool like a magnetic force. She didn't resist. She found herself succumbing to the will of the mob, her mind gradually accepting what was happening. As she relaxed, her body came to life with breathless sensitivity and shivers of carnality the likes of which she'd never before felt.

A narrow, curved bridge had been erected over the pool, with a small platform at the center. The exotic night lilies were in full bloom, a sweet-smelling forest of fanciful pink discs below. The crowd urged her forward, excitement nipping at everyone's heels. When she reached the platform, on cue the throng hushed. This was where she was to repeat the sacred incantations she'd memorized in the library.

As she did so, the crowd began to chant along, an eerie, dissonant harmony, their words and notes meshing in an extraordinary way with hers. Her mind spun, falling dizzily into unity with the collective. The sounds seeped into her consciousness, got tangled up in her ears and her mind, drawing her in deeper, somehow infusing her with their seductive meaning even though she didn't understand the language that was spoken.

Go to him
he who is bright with ten thousand
pleasures!

His fragrance of desire spreads like a
floodtide
drowning your eyes, and your head
whirls
as he drinks his fill…

Was she being hypnotized by the crowd? Or
bespelled…?

She lost all measure of time as they sang on
and on, a beautiful, lyrical prayer to their god
that he accept her blood sacrifice and shower
his blessings upon his faithful servants. All the
while her body hummed with a vivid, erotic vibration that aroused her senses to the point of
madness and made her ache to be part of the
roiling mass of bodies below, touching and tasting the drug of their immortality.

Or rather, one man's immortality.

The song called to her and her body answered
with a cry for Rhys. It was *him* she wanted.

She wanted to be a part of him, touching and
tasting the drowning sensations of the man she
loved.

She looked down at the people, searching
for him, knowing in her desperate heart she

wouldn't see him. But how she wished he would miraculously appear!

When you really need me, whisper my name. I'll be there to keep you safe.

But that wasn't possible. He was far away by now.

And she'd have to face this on her own.

Nephtys beckoned, and the *shemat*s led her over the bridge and down to the threshold of the inner sanctum, the holy of holies. The cave-dark chamber was alive with the glitter of two thousand tiny votive candles. The sweet spice of incense and ambergris and a thousand flowers wafted from the six side altars.

Her breath caught in her lungs.

An impossibly tall figure stood before the obsidian sarcophagus in the center, muscular and powerful, towering over everything around him. He looked like a huge statue of the god come to life. The brilliance of his raiment nearly blinded the eye. Diamonds covered his silver collar and black kilt, sparkling more brightly than the stars in the heavens he worshipped. The high, distinctive crown of Upper

Egypt shone like mother-of-pearl on his head, making him appear even more ominous.

He wore a half mask of silver, with lapis lazuli forming the elaborate eyes and hiding his features, but there was only one man it could be: the vampire High Priest Seth-Aziz. And he was truly magnificent.

She felt a deep shiver of unwilling and terrifying attraction low in her belly as he lifted his hand toward her.

"Come, my chosen one. Join the god and feed his hunger," his voice boomed, echoing through the courtyards of the temple like thunder.

The crowd urged her on. She didn't want to go.

Her knees trembled, her blood felt as insubstantial as faerie wings in her veins. She felt dizzy with fear.

Whisper my name. I'll be there.

"Rhys," she whispered, needing him desperately.

She felt a whir of magic within her heart at the sound of his name on her lips. Giving her the courage she needed.

The stern eyes behind the mask pinioned

her with their authority, willing her to obey and come to him. To release herself to his dominion.

It was impossible to resist his command. Of their own volition, her feet stepped over the threshold into the narrow chamber, and she went to stand before him. She closed her eyes and took his hand, swallowing heavily when his fingers closed around hers.

"My love," he said, the words low and filled with emotion. Her eyes shot open in shock.

She looked up at his face. And that's when she realized that the eyes looking back at her, shadowed by the mask, were not black, but the color of amber.

Rhys!

She opened her mouth to exclaim, but he bent to cover her lips with his, capturing her cry of joy and swallowing it as his own breath.

"Shh," he admonished into her mouth. "You must not give me away."

"But how—"

"The secret passage."

Her heart soared and quailed at the same time. "What about Seth?"

"Drugged. With a sleep herb from my garden."

He broke the kiss and straightened, leaving her breathless for more. She reached for him, and he took her in his embrace.

The crowd cheered its approval. The vampire had claimed his sacrificial vessel!

"Is it really you? This isn't some trick of magic?" she asked, terrified she was being deceived.

"It's really me, my darling."

Her body trembled to his touch, recognizing her lover by the tender way he held her, and by the subtle, earthy scent of al Fahl on his skin.

He raised a hand over her head, performing a thundering incantation over her and the immortals beyond.

"We must be gone before he awakes," he murmured as the crowd chanted a response. "An hour at most to complete the ceremony."

But the spell was real, and his power wove through the onlookers, spilling through her body like a fire-fall. She swayed and quickened with an intense surge of physical desire.

She caught sight of the huge altar behind him,

gleaming black and ready for her sacrifice. "But you're not a vampire…" she murmured breathlessly. Wishing for a split second he were…

He showed her a vial of blood secreted in his palm. "I've seen the ritual a hundred times and can do it in my sleep. The crowd will pay more attention to each other than to us, reveling in the pleasures of the magic."

In illustration, he threw out his hands and chanted a few words. Instantly, the air was charged with a thick current of carnal awareness.

"Oh!"

A shock of erotic sensation coursed through her body. He caught her hands as she reached out to steady herself. His touch sent her mind spinning, her body suddenly a mass of need.

For him.

She wanted to cry out his name, but stopped herself. "My lord!" she moaned instead. "Please!"

He continued to chant, and the throng of celebrants joined in with fevered enthusiasm as he unfastened the row of buttons down the front of the stole that covered her neck and shoulders. The hum of power around her leaped to a crescendo. It was blissful agony. She didn't think she could wait patiently while he finished taking off her wrap. She wanted to rip it off and grab him. *Make* him take her. His fingers brushed her naked skin, thrumming her arousal like sexual harp strings.

"Hurry," she urged. "Please hurry!"

He smiled, the architect of her body's capture, the sorcerer who'd enchanted her heart. She wanted his hands and his mouth on her. And his awesome power within her.

He slid the stole from her shoulders, baring her chest to his gaze and her throat to his bloody kiss. Her breasts rose and fell with her panting breath, the bodice of her gown far too tight against her aching nipples. She wanted him to tear it off her and take them in his mouth.

The crowd's chanting rose, urging the vampire to put his fangs to her neck and take his sacrifice. Excitement flushed through her, as his strong fingers grasped her arms, pulling her closer. His power was intoxicating, overwhelming; it flowed through her like potent liquor, robbing her of reason, making her flesh scream with need.

She knew she was bespelled; she didn't care. It felt too good.

"Do you give yourself to me?" he boomed so the restless, rowdy crowd could hear. "Do you wish to feed the god with your body and nurture him with your devotion?"

"Yes!" she answered, and with a shiver of surrender, she gave herself over to him.

He swept her up into his arms and carried her to the altar, where he laid her down. The black stone was slick and cool as ice against her bare back, and Rhys was hot, so hot, against her front as he mounted the altar and knelt over her.

He slid his hand behind her neck and lifted her upper body to press into his broad chest. His fingers brushed across the side of her throat, seeking the pulse. He bent over her and opened his mouth, licking a path along the throbbing vein he'd found. She burned with the contact, his tongue like a flame to her flesh. A flame of arousal.

His mouth opened wider and the edges of his teeth grazed her painfully sensitive skin. Erotic shivers cascaded through her breasts and down to the core of her need.

His eyes sought hers.

"Yes," she answered his unspoken question, needing him with every molecule in her body. "Do it."

His mouth closed around the flesh of her throat and he sucked. She felt a jolt of pleasure between her legs, like he was sucking her there. She moaned, tilting her head to give him better access. She felt boneless, helpless, at his complete mercy. His tongue flicked and she gasped, feeling the sensation on the nub throbbing painfully between her thighs.

His hand closed around her breast, his thumb rubbing her beaded nipple through the thin silk of her gown. He bent down to suck her there and she bowed up in intense pleasure, crying out. The first tingle of orgasm shimmered through her body.

"Don't stop," she begged. "Please don't stop!"

He tugged down the top of her bodice, grasping her taut nipples with relentless fingers, and returned his mouth to her throat. The quiver of climax blossomed, impossible to stop. She writhed under him. Reaching...reaching.

His teeth clamped around her frantically leaping pulse and he bit down, sucking hard as he squeezed her nipples. She screamed.

Orgasm seized her in its clutches and tore through her, throwing her entire being into a savage whirlwind of quivering, shaking, bone-melting pleasure.

And that's when she felt two sharp pricks biting deep into the flesh of her throat.

Fangs?

Her universe exploded into a gush of blood and another searing, mind-bending orgasm. But she had just enough presence of mind to think, oh, my God!

Had Seth awakened?

Chapter 21

While unhurried days come and go,
Let us turn to each other in quiet affection,
Walk in peace to the edge of old age.
—Song inscribed on an Earthen Vessel

Thankfully, by the time Rhys concluded the ritual act, his immortal peers were deep into lascivious celebration. Gillian had fainted, overcome by the drowning erotic power she'd been deluged with at the end. And possibly by shock. She hadn't been expecting the fangs.

Even though his own body still buzzed dangerously from the experience, craving release, he could not delay their departure. He leaped from the altar, scooped her into his arms, and wove quickly through the crush of revelers, back through the temple to Seth's dressing room.

He adjusted her body in his arms to close the door behind them, and her eyelashes fluttered open. She gazed up at him, her expressive green eyes still glazed with a lingering haze of pleasure.

"Rhys?" she asked, her voice uncertain.

"Shh. We need to be quiet," he said, glancing around to make sure they were alone. "Unless you wish Seth to awaken and find us. I assure you, he won't be in a very good mood when he does."

"So…" she whispered hoarsely. Her fingers went to the wound on her neck and her gaze to his mouth. Her face had drained of color. "You're a vampire?"

He could feel the warm stickiness of the blood that had spilled from his lips and down his chin. Her blood. And his own, which he had gathered in the vial and used to make the bite appear more realistic.

The fangs were gone, but the taste of her lingered on his tongue. The air charged between them, and he looked down at her, still hot and needy. She had found release. He hadn't.

But this wasn't the time. They must move quickly.

"No." He set her onto a divan, pulled off his mask and crown and tossed them aside. "I'm a shape-shifter. You know that."

"You had fangs," she said, meeting his eyes accusingly.

He probably should have warned her about that part.

"An illusion spell. I wasn't sure if it would work," he said, and cast a hurried look behind the dressing screen in the corner to make sure Seth hadn't stirred. He was still sprawled on the floor where he'd collapsed after drinking the drugged wine Rhys had sneaked in and left earlier.

I'm sorry, my friend. You gave me no choice.

Gillian had sat up and was peering at the wounds on her neck in a hand mirror. "You're saying these aren't real?"

"The fangs were illusion, but the effect they had was not. Come. We must hurry."

He found the hidden lever and opened the low door to the other secret passage she had discovered on the map. He'd been exploring the tunnels for the past two days, pretending to be resigned to his confinement to his rooms, while he was in reality plotting and gathering the supplies they would need for their journey.

"We're covered in blood," she said, rising to follow him. "We'll scare anyone who sees us."

"I have water to wash and a change of clothes hidden in the old tomb," he told her.

She took his hand as he was about to usher her into the darkness of the narrow passage. "Are you sure, Rhys?"

He sensed the deeper meaning behind the question, and felt the connection between them even more strongly. He wanted this woman. Wanted her in every way a man could want a woman. He wanted to love her and make love to her, cherish her and grow old with her. He lifted her hand and kissed her fingers. "Never more sure of anything in my life."

Then he led his woman down into the yawning, black portal toward an uncertain fate.

In the ancient tomb of Seth-Aziz where they'd first met, they cleaned up and he helped her into the masculine head-to-toe Bedouin garb he had chosen as her disguise. That's when Gillian suddenly noticed the slight change in the inscription that covered the wall of the tomb. In the scene of Seth-Aziz worshipping Set-Sutekh along with his *shemsu,* another figure now kneeled next to Lord Rhys Kilpatrick. A woman. A blonde. And the name inscribed next to it was Gillian's own.

She stared at it, startled. "I suppose they'll chisel us out now," she said at length. Surprised at the sting of regret she felt.

"Perhaps," he said, and kissed her. "Their loss."

"Will you shift?" she asked, smiling.

He smiled back and kissed her again. "Yes. So I can be between your thighs as we ride the wind."

"Where will we go?" she asked as they

stepped out into the pale light of the breaking dawn.

He looked toward the east, to the ribbon of silver-green water, the river that gave this land life. Beyond, the golden disc of the sun broke through above the ragged tear of the horizon, piercing its rays into the peaceful darkness, stabbing out the stars with its bright light, waking the valley to its day of toil and strife.

He turned away and looked toward the north.

"Petru," she said, following his gaze.

She had done her homework, it seemed. He glanced at her and shook his head. "No. It's where they'll expect us to go."

"It's where you can remain immortal."

"That doesn't matter," he said. "I want to grow old with you."

"You said it wouldn't be a betrayal to join Haru-Re. You said you could work for the good of Khepesh, even in the camp of the enemy."

"That was before I had you with me," he said. "It's too dangerous."

"I'd like to see my mother again," she said quietly.

He took her in his arms and held her close. And knew he must do this for her, so she could have peace in her heart. He kissed her hair. "Very well. Petru it is, then."

She tilted up her face and gazed at him with her beautiful green eyes. There was so much love in them it humbled him. He would do anything for her. Anything in the world to keep that adoring look in her eyes.

"It'll be fine," she said. "You'll see."

"You're not afraid?" he asked.

"No." She rested her cheek against his chest. "I know I'll be safe with you."

"You will," he vowed. "And you'll be mine forever. We'll find the spell to make it so, I promise you. Because I intend to keep you for at least that long."

"And I'll cherish every minute we have together. Oh, Rhys, I'm so happy."

"I love you," he said, and kissed her smiling lips.

"I love you, too," she said, and his heart swelled.

He shifted to al Fahl and she climbed on his

back, and together they rode off into the desert, the ghost stallion and his mortal mate.

And their love would last until the end of time.

Epilogue

I'd stop her passage,
hold her for questioning,
then sit to enjoy the range of her voice
as she raged like a fury on and on.
                                    —Papyrus Harris 500

Nephtys swept into Seth's dressing room, grabbing a goblet of wine from a table by the door as she passed by. "Sweet Isis, *that* was some performance, my brother," she announced, somewhat surprised, but with no small amount of gratification. "I told you your intended

would come around. Merciful Min, she was
practically—"

She halted in midsentence when she realized no one was listening. "Seth?" she asked.
Her puzzled query was answered with a pained
moan from…the floor behind the dressing
screen.

"Hadu!" She set down the wine and rushed
to his side. "By the stars of Nut, what happened
to you? Are you hurt?"

He groaned as he struggled to sit up. "Only
my pride. And my head," he amended, pressing his fingers into his temples and massaging
them. "I swear to Sekhmet, if I ever catch that
accursed Englishman, I'll…"

"Shall I call the guards?" she asked anx-
iously when his words trailed off into another
moan.

"No. Just Shahin. No one else."

She stuck her head out the door and called
for the sheikh to be brought.

"What do you mean, catch the Englishman?"
she persisted. "I thought Kilpatrick was confined to his rooms."

That's when she noticed that her brother was

wearing only his linen undergarments. "Oh, dear," she said with a prickle of foreboding.

"What the hell happened here?" The sheikh stole the words from her lips when he strode in and saw her expression along with Seth's state.

"The ceremony," Seth said, allowing Shahin to help him to his divan. "It wasn't me. It was Rhys."

Nephtys's eyes widened. "Well! That explains Lady Gillian's sudden turnaround in affections. But how on earth did he manage to overpower you?"

"His Sufi knockout herb," Shahin guessed, and Seth nodded.

"I should have anticipated the move," he said. "But I was frankly expecting him to take her *during* the ceremony, not before it."

Nephtys blinked at him. "You were *expecting* to be attacked?" she asked incredulously. "And did nothing about it?"

"He didn't attack me. He drugged me. And carried out the ritual to perfection, I gather."

Shahin scowled. "Down to the bite. They were quite convincing, he and the woman. His powers are far greater than any of us guessed.

He will be a danger to Khepesh now." This last Shahin said with profound regret in his voice. He started for the door. "I'll have the gates sealed."

"Too late. They are long gone by now. They found the ancient hidden passages."

Shahin's eyes narrowed. "Then I'll mount a search. He won't dare go to his estate. And he won't have gotten far in the desert carrying the woman."

"No." Seth got to his feet, and Nephtys hurried to offer her supporting arm. "No search. Let them go."

"You can't mean that, *hadu!* What they have done is unforgivable. Both should rightly be put to death."

"Which is exactly why we must let them escape."

She exchanged a look of dismay with Shahin, who just looked pensive. "Does this Sufi herb muddle one's judgment after rendering one unconscious?" she asked him in alarm.

Shahin turned a thoughtful gaze to Seth. "Not to my knowledge."

"Seth!" she exclaimed, wanting to knock

the sense back into the man that the herb had knocked out. "You know they'll head straight for Petru. Right into the welcoming arms of our enemy!"

She gasped in dismay as she remembered her vision. The one where Rhys Kilpatrick was doing just that, being greeted by a smug and smiling Haru-Re. The vision was coming true!

"With any luck," Seth murmured, bringing her back to the present with a jolt.

She froze, her mouth dropping open in shock. "*Hadu,* what are you saying?" she whispered.

A forbidding smile played with the corners of Shahin's mouth. "What he's saying, my lady…is that he planned this."

She searched her brother's face and found the terrible truth written there. Her blood chilled at the immense danger he had deliberately put them all in. "Does he know?" she asked hoarsely. "Kilpatrick. Did you plan it with him? Or are you just hoping he's as loyal as you want to believe?"

He put his arm around her shoulder and gave her an affectionate kiss on the cheek. "You tell me, my sister. Look into your scrying bowl and tell me if I've misjudged the honor of my friend."

She did not want to let it drop, but she could tell he was weary and his head was hurting. "By the gods, you are impossible," she said with a mixture of love, exasperation and profound worry. "This cannot end well."

"Only the future will tell."

"And what of the Lady Gillian?" she asked sadly. "She was to be your greatest love. The wise consort all of Khepesh would look up to in years to come. You've let her slip through your fingers!"

Her brother sighed. "Sometimes the best way to win a woman over is to let her follow where her heart leads her. If she is truly meant to be mine, her heart will bring her back to me."

She was about to protest his ridiculously faulty reasoning, but Shahin strode toward the door, reminding her of his presence. "In the meantime," he said, ever the practical one, "you will need another sacrifice as soon as possible. I shall go and try to find someone appropriate."

"Be discreet," Nephtys told him. "Seek

her aboveground. We don't want it known the ceremony was a fake."

Seth raised a hand. "Wait."

Shahin halted, hand on the door. "You have a preference, my lord?"

"Perhaps." Seth narrowed his eyes. "Do you still have that note Miss Haliday wrote to her sisters?"

The sheikh patted his robes. "Still right here, as you ordered."

"Well," the high priest of Khepesh said with a slow, calculating smile. "I think it's time to deliver it, don't you?"

* * * * *

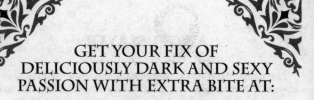

MILLS & BOON

are proud to present our...

Book of the Month

Sins of the Flesh
by Eve Silver

from Mills & Boon® Nocturne™

Calliope and soul reaper Mal are enemies, but as
they unravel a tangle of clues, their attraction grows.
Now they must choose between loyalty to those
they love, or loyalty to each other—to the one
they each call enemy.

Available 4th March

*Something to say about our Book of the Month?
Tell us what you think!*

millsandboon.co.uk/community
facebook.com/romancehq
twitter.com/millsandboonuk

WELCOME TO PENANCE, OHIO—
HELL ON EARTH!

"Jennifer Armintrout always delivers!"
—GENA SHOWALTER

Graf's stuck in a town where no one enters…
and no one leaves.

As a vampire Graf's free to indulge his every dark, dangerous
and debauched whim. He was just looking for a good
party, until a road trip detour trapped him in
the cursed town of Penance.

The eerie hamlet affects Graf in ways he never expected
and he soon finds himself going against his very nature
to protect town outcast Jessa from a sinister attack.

Keeping her safe is a surprising impulse, yet working with
the human girl could be Graf's only hope of breaking the
spell that binds the town. That is, *if* he can keep his
lethal urges and deadly desires under control.

FREE BOOK
AND A SURPRISE GIFT

We would like to take this opportunity to thank you for reading this Mills & Boon® book by offering you the chance to take a specially selected book from the Nocturne™ series absolutely FREE! We're also making this offer to introduce you to the benefits of the Mills & Boon® Book Club™—

- **FREE home delivery**
- **FREE gifts and competitions**
- **FREE monthly Newsletter**
- **Exclusive Mills & Boon Book Club offers**
- **Books available before they're in the shops**

Accepting this FREE book and gift places you under no obligation to buy, you may cancel at any time, even after receiving your free book. Simply complete your details below and return the entire page to the address below. You don't even need a stamp!

YES Please send me a free Nocturne book and a surprise gift. I understand that unless you hear from me, I will receive 3 superb new stories every month, two priced at £4.99 and a third larger version priced at £6.99, postage and packing free. I am under no obligation to purchase any books and may cancel my subscription at any time. The free book and gift will be mine to keep in any case.

Ms/Mrs/Miss/Mr _____ Initials _____

Surname _____

Address _____

_____ Postcode _____

E-mail _____

Send this whole page to: Mills & Boon Book Club, Free Book Offer, FREEPOST NAT 10298, Richmond, TW9 1BR